Rubicon

By

Ian Patrick

Fahrenheit Press

For Emma, from your man of few words,

Never wear slippers to a shoeing. Ben Hamer should have listened to this advice but he didn't. Big H is down two million. Now, Hamer is no fool. He's a Yank and works with money. The only issue is, he should have invested in property as Big H had requested. But he hadn't. That's where I come in.

I'm not affiliated to the big man but I have been subcontracted, on a few occasions, to rectify business transactions that have gone awry. It's quite a simple contract; whatever you borrow you must give back with the agreed interest. Hamer is Big H's accountant. He'd done good work until he decided to work both ends of the chain and start talking to the old bill about Big H's money. You see, even amongst criminals there's a code of conduct. Hamer has breached that line.

I have nothing to do with either of them but I do have my own set of morals. Morals are the Velcro of society. I see myself as a twenty-first century bounty hunter. In my work the first law of survival is to stay alive. The first rule of any hunt: Don't be seen. This applies to the hunted as well as the hunter, that's why I've been so successful. I've never met Big H but he knows how to get hold of me.

In the end it's about discipline and Hamer lacks it. I was raised on discipline; something my old man was keen on. I've the buckle scars on my back to prove it. My mum also took her fair share. She shouldn't have intervened.

Childhood prepared me for the army. When I left the service, I was educated for life. Her Majesty also prepared me to kill; another bonus. Second rule: Know your target. The army was keen on this message as friendly fire is frowned upon.

When you're getting paid to do a job, do it properly. Now this wasn't too difficult with Hamer. He'd met me but wouldn't remember me. I knew Big H didn't want this done as a knock on the door. This isn't an Ikea self-build. The instructions must be clear.

Following him was a piece of piss. He's an accountant, not a villain. Hamer is slower than an amputeed sloth and this made following him simple. His portly frame exuded an odour that was distinguishable in crowds. He would stop frequently. This is easy to combat on a foot follow but tougher by vehicle. Hamer was often looking over his shoulder when he was out on the capital's streets, but then, who isn't in London? Hamer wasn't aware of me.

I know this as I've given up my cab for him and sat in the same food joints as him. He's oblivious to his surroundings. I dress up to dress down because it helps in the hunt and fits with the first rule: Don't be seen. I can adapt in most places. I'm in an age bracket where you take a pride in yourself but no one really notices you.

Money hasn't changed him. Hamer sticks with habitual routes, uses cabs and avoids public transport. His size and his apathy for exercise means he stops frequently. He ends up in the same place most lunch times, a small garden area in Temple, protected by Chambers. He enjoys foot-long meatball subs. The juices leak from his mouth like drool from a hippo. It took a month to learn his rituals, his lunch spot and his favourite titty bar. You may have money, work with money and wipe your arse with money but when it's not your money, you can't hide or keep the change.

I've rented a room in a converted courthouse in Elephant and Castle. It houses a bunch of Buddhists on retreat. I sleep in what was a holding cell but has now been appropriately redecorated and the lock is now on the inside. It's sparse but there's a certain beauty in minimalism. This works well for me. No one speaks or asks questions, there's no CCTV and I can meditate.

Meditation calms the mind. Teaches me patience, a necessary trait when you're about to end a life. Remember the second rule: Know your target, mistakes cost lives.

I know where Hamer will be in the next hour, it's a Thursday so he'll be at the titty bar. He'll be dressed in his only grey pinstripe suit, his trousers held up by braces that strain against his gut like a noose on a neck. He'll leave around midnight and I know what route he'll take to get home. I take my time getting ready. It's easy in this small abode. I've chosen a black tracksuit, dark polo sweater and black peaked cap. I have the appearance of a running insomniac, which should blend in well with the surroundings and the route I'll be taking to Hamer's final destination. There's a peaceful serenity about the Centre, a 'calm abiding', they call it. I feel it but not enough to stop me.

I leave the Centre and turn left onto the main drag to Elephant and Castle. At the lights I cross and avail myself of the London Bike scheme. The one thing this government has enabled is state-endorsed crime. Santander may sponsor the bike but that's not the message being 'pedalled'. I cannot tell you the amount of pushers I know who use this service to transport their commodities about the London streets, providing the poor unfortunate masses with their fast food. Big H controls their financial sector. He also provides the payment to facilitate the hire. A generous man.

The traffic over Blackfriars Bridge is sedate and I'm making good time. I travel light; a small compact backpack is all I need to carry my tools. Hamer is getting his fill at the bar and not all of it drink. I know from my times sitting opposite him that he'll be playing with change in his pocket whilst he wipes his sweat-strewn brow with a handkerchief that has seen better days. He consumes neat whiskey and tips the ladies well. They in turn allow him a quick feel but nothing more.

I've become friendly with the inevitable although I don't wish to meet my maker anytime soon. Looking at my watch face I am aware that I am the only person who knows Hamer's time is coming to an end – unless of course you believe in God, which I don't.

I picked Thursday for his demise, as I knew he would have enjoyed his last hours before death. I could afford him this last luxury. I am a decent man after all. Big H sees it differently, which he can; it was his money Hamer gambled with.

The ride along Pentonville Road is tough and the climb steep from King's Cross. I remember life is tougher with every revolution of the wheel. I replace the bike at a docking station near Chapel Market and begin my run. I check my watch, a 'Rolex' purchased on a beach in Thailand. The watch is fake but it provides genuine time.

It's 0030 hours. I have twenty minutes.

Barnsbury, respite for the hip and bohemian. An area populated by politicians and the head of a prominent crime family. It's also where Hamer has chosen to rent a one-bedroom ground-floor studio flat. The curtains still twitch here. First rule: Don't be seen. Even in a salubrious area the street lighting is poor and provides me with good cover. I pause by the steps of 62A and undo the backpack. Only four steps from street to door. The basement flat is vacant.

The petrol-filled water bottle I'd been carrying gradually becomes lighter as I thoughtfully dispense its toxic smelling contents over the front door and main step. If anyone were looking they would just see a man emptying a bottle after his run. The streets are quiet, the only visitor an urban fox who has the sense and wisdom not to approach. I smile at him. Many a time I would be lying in a hedgerow waiting for my foe and a fox would stroll by, take a piss on me and move on. A rare skill to be invisible to the indigenous street dweller. I'm careful not to get any petrol inside the letterbox. Insurance is high in this area. Time 0040 hours. Hamer will be here in five. I carry on pouring the petrol down the steps and across the road where I stop at the entrance to a small secluded park.

A pair of eyes catches my attention and I freeze. The same hunters' eyes I had seen earlier watching and waiting for any spoils. Headlights sweep through the park and I duck back. I remove a Zippo from my pocket. I hear the vehicle stop. The engine remains running. It's a black cab. I know the engine noise. I hear Hamer's voice and I move forward towards the gate to the park entrance. Voices emanate and formalities are exchanged. Only two voices, both male. The night is pleasant with very little breeze.

The eyes that were following me have disappeared. This is it. I am about to cross the Rubicon. I pull my polo neck over my lower face and my cap peak down. My gloves feel like skin and the grip on the lighter is good. Tick, tick goes the watch. The flame ignites with the first flick of my thumb. I move towards the end of the fuel line and look up with one final check. I hear another engine, not a car. Hamer turns towards me and his eyes briefly catch mine. I sense a glimmer of recognition then he looks away in the direction of the road. I freeze. Darkness turns to light and he's gone. Lit up like a self-immolating monk.

The scene has altered now. Police tape decorates the road at either end. A white tent has been erected thirty feet from the flat's charred door. A 500cc Kawasaki motorbike lies on its side further along the road. A black cab with its passenger door missing is emanating smoke into the night air and misting the portable lights. Fire has devoured it. Three fire trucks remain, engines idling. The low hum of the generator ticks over and illuminates people in white suits and masks, some on their hands and knees, picking at the road and moving in one horizontal line, others coming in and out of the main door to the flat.

The smell of petrol is overpowering, which is fortuitous, as I haven't changed clothing. There are no ambulances, only local voyeurs. I've always enjoyed this moment, the return to the scene of the crime. The creation of chaos is an occupational hazard but one that keeps many in employment.

A uniformed police officer stands by the scene tape looking bored. At least he's had the heat of the fire to keep him warm. I decide to approach, I've seen what I need to see. My polo neck is rolled down and my hat on as befits the situation. I reach into my right pocket. As I approach, the uniform officer moves forward to stop me but is intercepted by a young female wearing a forensic suit. Her auburn hair is tied back in a ponytail; she doesn't wear makeup and looks tired.

She moves in front of the uniform and takes a clipboard from him. I continue forward and stop at the edge of the line. Some rules are vital to obey, implied or otherwise. She approaches me, confidence emanates from her protective garment.

"Looks like the bike rider lost control, mounted the pavement and killed the male as he was getting out the cab. The rider went over the top of the bike in a ball of flame. Petrol from the bike engine ignited them both. The corpse we've established is a Ben Hamer. Next of kin informed but there's not much of him to be identified. Motorcyclist is at UCH, not likely to survive. I've requested pre-transfusion blood and started house to house. Cab driver is giving a statement. It's all in hand, sarge."

I nod, sign the crime scene log, hang my warrant card round my neck and duck under the tape. A forensic suit and shoes are handed to me. Final rule: Keep your enemies close. They're your greatest teacher.

Let me explain how I came to be here. To do that I need to fill in some back story.

<u>Sensitive log entry – 0800 hours 10th August 2020</u>

This is the sensitive decision log for DCI Klara Winter.

All entries will be made by me and no other person. I will record both views and thoughts of individuals and the on-going enquiry.

I will not be disclosing this record to the defence as it contains sensitive information pertaining to covert methods. The CPS will guide me when and if required.

This log is concerned with Operation Storm, a National Crime Agency enquiry into a subject known as Vincenzo Guardino, aka Big H and his associates, concerned in the importation of class A drugs and firearms to the UK.

It will detail my thoughts and decisions concerning covert assets and their use during this enquiry.

This is a major enquiry and will use the HOLMES system for recording actions and all non-sensitive records relating to the operation.

I am short staffed, but who isn't? I have requested more staff but will have to wait to see how the investigation progresses in this lifestyle phase.

I am satisfied I can continue at this time without jeopardising officer safety.

Log started in relation to secondment of an undercover officer (UCO) from the Metropolitan Police Covert Intelligence Command Anti-Terrorist Command (SCO35).

This has NOT been requested by myself and is NOT wanted in relation to this investigation.

I have sufficient cover, at present, in relation to the target that would NOT warrant the use of a UCO employed direct into the organised criminal network.

I have been called this morning by Commander Helen Barnes, Metropolitan Police Service Covert Intelligence Command, and been directed that the UCO will be employed on my operation as to a wider remit of national security the reasons for which I will NOT be briefed on.

The UCO is DS Sam Batford.

I don't understand who the fuck she thinks she is, foisting this methodology on me at this stage in the investigation, and have no alternative course of action I can take.

DS Batford will meet with me later today where he will be left in no uncertain terms as to my displeasure at their arrival and my expectations of being kept updated as to their findings in the course of my enquiry.

I feel my inclusion on the fast track promotion scheme and recent promotion to DCI is irksome to the MPS and Commander Barnes.

All funding, in relation to the UCO, will be met by SCO35 – MPS and as far as I'm concerned, they will be lucky to get a cup of tea out of me.

Entry complete.
DCI Winter
Senior Investigating Officer
Op Storm

2

Major Crime. That's my business. A month previously I was seconded to the National Crime Agency. For an elite lot of staff their anonymity is poor. I approach my new offices in Spring Gardens SE11 and the National Crime Agency sign greets me. I'd looked the address up online. I had visited when it was the Serious Organised Crime Agency. I stop, take a look. It's important to know your surroundings before you go waltzing in. The double security gates contain a vehicle in the tiger trap. A blue Ford Mondeo, blacked out rear windows. As one door shuts the other opens. It exits right.

My entrance is through metal side doors. An air lock lets me in and spews me out. A reception officer looks up, I move towards him. The fella on the desk looks at my warrant card then at me. He hands the card back, picks up a phone and dials an internal number. His worn, nicotine-stained fingers stab at the keypad.

"Your man's here."

He nods at me to sit as he replaces the receiver. I stay standing. He feels like king of his domain but he needs to know who's really in control.

It was the same in the army. When you were on point you coveted it. You owned the area despite being near the unknown. No matter what the rank, you did your role until you were instructed otherwise. The difference in civvy street is there's no discipline. We're all laws unto ourselves when the chips are down. 'Fools Gold' chimes its announcement from my inner pocket; the Nokia 3210 vibrates in synchronicity. I let the tune ring on a while. I love it. It means work and gives me time to prepare an answer.

I press green and hold the phone to my ear. Never speak until you've heard the voice at the other end. The wrong voice could cost lives. Some phones you should never lose and this was one of them.

"Alright, babes? I heard you was back. I need a meet."

I know the voice. I should do, I recruited her. I check the Home Office-issue clock on the reception wall. I breathe and bide my time.

"Seven p.m., outside Mount Pleasant Sorting Office."

I terminate the call. I've got enough time to make my introductions here, conduct the meet and greet then get to my main work. She knew I was in the UK as I'd left a calling card at her address. She doesn't need to know how I knew it. If she asks then it's word of mouth on her estate rather than a voters' check on our systems and a fake call to the local authority housing department regarding a noise complaint.

Now, don't get me wrong, I love society and all the good it brings. I may come across like an uncaring callous bastard but for the record I do have a heart and I'm good at what I get paid to do. I just have high expectations. The goods are what it's all about in this world. We order on-line and have an expectation that the parcel will arrive well packaged and at the agreed location and time. I am one such package. I get a call told what the order is and the boss expects delivery, on time and with the minimum of fuss. Some orders are easy to complete but this one is going to be a bitch.

From the reflection in the one-way glass I can see a female, early thirties, auburn hair, slim fit grey trousers and white shirt open at the neck. She speaks with the guard and he nods in my direction. She approaches me and I wait to turn. She's confident, self-assured and I already know she's the detective chief inspector of the unit I'm seconded to. I turn and get in first.

"DS Batford, ma'am. Pleased to meet you."

She doesn't shake hands. An interesting first response.

"Morning, Batford. DCI Winter. Let's get you to your office, shall we? You can meet the others and get yourself settled in. We're in the middle of a job as I know you're aware."

She walks towards an inner door, swipes her card and the lock disengages. I follow. The stark white of the halogen-illuminated corridor contrasts well with her outfit. From her tan she's clearly just back from holiday or she has her own glow tube.

Thick, soundproof doors encase rooms off the corridor. All key coded. She says nothing, just pushes open double doors until we go up a flight of stairs. Six flights. She also loves fitness. The lifts were good. I've learnt that the best approach in these situations is to mirror the other's actions. I say nothing. Bide my time, calm my nerves and follow her arse up to room 320A.

No signs alert you to who resides in each office. Need to know – and I don't need to know. As she covers the keypad from me I can hear MAARS's *Pump up the Volume* being played on the other side. The first door opens into a small corridor. Small metal lockers adorn the wall. They're the kind you see in a John Lewis store where you can leave your phone and charge it whilst spending your hard-earned cash on items you never needed or thought of until you entered. You have the key to retrieve your property and with a full battery, message all on Facebook and Twitter with numerous smiley emoticons and photos of your shit.

"Turn off your phones. All of them. Put them in there and take a key."

I do as directed, on this occasion. The SIM card from both phones already rest in my wallet, I'd removed in reception. She swipes into another door pad and the music increases in volume as the door opens.

"Turn that shit off," she directs, as she breezes in. An

overweight male, late forties, bald with goatee, flicks the radio off.

I don't wait to be invited in. The room is relatively silent. It's a typical squad office, all Superdry tops and stubble. The only two females look at me, their eyes follow as I enter the goldfish bowl. Ma'am's office. She locks the door and shuts the blinds. This is getting interesting.

"I'll be brief."

She smooths her trousers and sits behind her mediocre melamine desk. Standard size, scratch-resistant covering. The chair isn't. It's bespoke, Occupational Health-measured and issued. She has a back problem. I get seated whilst she ignores me and checks her computer. She puts on glasses and leans into the screen.

"Is that it?" I ask.

She opens a drawer and takes out a thick file. My personnel file. She opens it and I can make out the first photo taken when you join the force stapled to the flap. It's called a service now. Force appeared too authoritarian and strong. I prefer Force. It adds weight, and does the public really give a shit what terminology we use? The DCI takes a breath as she's about to speak.

"I haven't even started, Batford. I don't welcome secondments and I certainly don't welcome secondments from Specialist Operations Undercover Unit. We investigate national major crime involving guns, drugs and organised criminal networks. We're in the middle of the biggest investigation into an OCN ever conducted in this country. Last thing I need is to babysit you."

She pauses as she flicks through my file. She thinks she's smart because she has it. She knows this display will make me uneasy. Make me believe she has access to higher authorities that release such material. What she doesn't know is that my original file was shredded. How do I know? I did it. The one I replaced it with is perfectly acceptable and could be corroborated. Fools rush in where wise men never go. I say nothing. I know this game. I've been here before.

No squad relishes outsiders coming in. Especially ones that will be amongst the people they're looking at. I say nothing until the moment comes to speak. That won't be long.

Thirty seconds.

"So you were born in nineteen seventy-eight, parents unknown. Taken straight into care at birth and placed in foster care where you remained on long-term placement until you joined the army in nineteen ninety-four and saw undisclosed active service."

I wait for her to ask where and which regiment but she has the common sense to not go there. She's loving every minute of it. It's clear by the way her eyes strain over the top of her glasses that perch on the lower bridge of her nose. I can take it. I wrote it and so far it's true. In fact all she will read out is. Why shouldn't it be? It makes interesting reading. I say nothing and wait patiently for her to carry on.

"Left the army in two thousand one to join the Metropolitan Police where you served in uniform in Tottenham. Did your round of promotion and squads and ended up in The Covert Intelligence Command as an undercover officer where you've been to date."

She shuts the file, takes off her glasses and rubs her nose. I've had enough. I start a slow handclap. It's all I can think of to break the ice.

"Feel better now? I'm here because of who you're investigating. You glanced over my detective career because it pisses on yours. You're a fast-track promotion, on your third marriage and have no kids. Your life is over. The NCA is your family and not a close one at that. Your team leach ambivalence towards you, as they know you've not worked the main squads. I've seen it from both sides of the fence. I'm here because the powers that be don't want this fucking up. I didn't ask for it, I was sent. Quite frankly I don't know you and didn't see fit to pull your file to find out. Word of mouth was all I needed. You either work with me or against me I don't care but you have to use me. Your call, ma'am."

I sit back, she stands up. I'm five foot eleven. She can't

dominate me.

"I've worked for three months on this. If I needed UCO input I would have requested it. This lot aren't tree hugging activists you can just shack up with and shag to get the information. We're not talking about some power station being taken over by a bunch of fucking hippies, sergeant."

Mirroring language. So old school. I have no interest in her job, only an aspect of it. MAC-10 machine pistols, to be precise. Some will go to proper villains but others will end up with local gangs to unleash on the capital's streets. Not sexy stuff, I know, and not terrorist related but they will make a nasty mess, send murder rates sky high and not be good for the economic well-being of the country. How do I know this is the case? I've been told. Chance conversations are so underrated. I also know the amount of cocaine that comes with them but I'm curious to see if she knows first.

"You'll be working to my directive, Batford. If you stray from it I'll have you back at the airport checking passports. I've spoken with your unit and they will provide your cover officer. I don't want he or she anywhere near my plot either. Is that clear?"

"Crystal."

That was quicker than I'd thought.

She slides a piece of paper across the desk and I take it. It's a memorandum of understanding, or MOU in the trade. I scan it. It makes no odds what's in it; I've breached it before it was printed. I sign it with my warrant number and slide it back with the Bic biro. The understanding is clear. Don't speak with anyone outside the room about the job. Bit difficult though. I'm already wrapped up in it.

She places the MOU in her desk tray then hands me another.

"It's an inclusion notice. Sign it and you get briefed as to where we are now. Don't sign it and you can fuck off out of this building."

I take it. It's basic. A standard template. No conditions. A rookie mistake. I take out my Mont Blanc pen and sign in the same way. She takes it back and looks at the numbers. She makes sure it's identical on both documents.

I need to build some trust. Trust is key. Without trust you have no momentum, no will to progress. I can't do anything until she confirms who she's looking at and for what purpose. I also need to know how she's getting the information. I've been told what I have to do and that's to recover the guns. A hundred weapons is a big ask. First you have to find them, persuade the owner to let them go and then get them to the mainland unnoticed. I do know that criminals have a tendency to over-egg the omelette and that a hundred is more than likely ten. Money is due to go across and a hundred is expected. I know this as my firm have told me so. The accountant of the recipient is also rumoured to be talking to police. Loose lips sink ships. I hope he's checked the lifeboats because his ship has started taking on water. The captain of that ship is Ben Hamer.

She's by my chair now. Her perfume smells like it needs changing. That stale scent that shows a will to make the effort but doesn't have the time. I get up.

"Shall we?" She motions to the door and we step into the main office. It's busier now. People have returned. The smell of fish and chips dominates the room. It's a small squad. It should be one detective inspector, a detective sergeant and eight detective constables. There's only the DS and five DCs as an outside team. The DI is on sick leave a DC is on maternity leave. These things seem mundane but to me this information is key. I need to know who I'm up against on the outside. The players I don't mind. They don't have the support of the old bill; well, not officially.

She claps her hands and they stop what they're doing and turn towards us. I lean up against a grey steel filing cabinet.

"This is our secondment from the Met's SCO35Unit. He's been sent here to provide UCO cover for our job."

The team's mouths open like a gathering of prostitutes at an orgy. I'd spotted the DS; he was the one that went to get up but was restrained by a helpful hand on his arm.

"I can see what you all think of this but we have no choice. We are at a crucial stage in the development of this work. I want you to see this as an opportunity. Briefing room please, and let's get up to date."

Chairs shuffle and paperwork is locked away. Trust is going to be tough here. I wait for them to enter the briefing room adjacent to the DCI's office. Comfy set-up. Armchairs, coffee machine, an overhead projector. I notice the camera above a TV for outside briefings. I take my seat at the back and wait as the DCI brings down a ceiling-mounted power screen. She logs into a computer and the NCA emblem flashes up. We're off. Hardest part done. I'm in, no real drama just minor discomfort. Like a leper walking into a spa.

"I'm DCI three-two-seven-eight. This briefing is being audio recorded and relates to Operation Storm, an Intelligence-led operation targeting Vincenzo Guardino, also known as Big H. Guardino is one the biggest importers of cocaine and heroin in Europe. We know he's planning an imminent importation of a hundred kilos of cocaine. He has many money laundering enterprises and his books are kept by an American called Ben Hamer."

I look at the covert image of Hamer flash up on the screen. It's recent. He still has a tan. The DCI used her warrant number in the introduction. No name. She fears this network and rightly so. Briefing documents change hands for good money. I've sold a few.

"Next up is Guardino."

The DCI has relaxed. "He's our main target. We know where he lives, works and that he has a chauffeur. He keeps clean. He even has a TV licence. Surveillance picked him up this weekend meeting Hamer and an unidentified white female at Heathrow Airport. The female and Guardino are known to each other. She has been seen with him on previous occasions. I need her identified and fast. Is she a courier? Secretary? What is her association with our target?"

Bingo. "I'll take that action," I shout, from the back, so I'm heard. Game on. She glances to the DS who shrugs and nods back. Such subservience to lower ranks breeds contempt. Displays a clear lack of authority. What she *should* have done was tell me she hadn't finished the briefing; all questions and assignments would be divvied up at the end. This operation is confidential. Any task or action is written out and given to an officer to resolve and feedback the outcome. Better for me not to have a computer involved. Data tracking is not my best friend. I need anonymity.

"Very well. Speak to DS Hudson after."

I nod. She carries on.

"What we also know is he's planning an importation of firearms along with the drugs. We have no timescale."

The more I listen, the less faith I have this team will bring it to fruition. The benefit is that the DCI will find me indispensable. The briefing was short. They've made little progress beyond housing Guardino and Hamer. Lifestyle work takes time. Progress can be slow when they don't come out to play. My firm knew this. That's why they sent me in. My bosses need the delivery to take place. There are buyers lined up hungry for food. They may be coppers but they know buyers don't wait.

The briefing comes to a swift end. There's no more to say. They have as much information as a traffic warning sign. You know there may be trouble ahead, what that could be is anyone's guess. I'm the last to leave the room. Shunned like a vegan at a hog roast. DS Hudson is sitting back at his desk. All clear of paperwork and extraneous stationery. I approach and he has the good sense to hold out his hand.

"Danny Hudson."

He has a weak handshake.

"Bring me up to speed on what you need. I can't be long -- I've a deployment in an hour."

Blatant lie. Makes me sound indispensable and adds an air of secrecy that all cops love. I have to eat and change for the seven p.m. meet with Miss Stone. The team's most wanted.

Hudson is in his early thirties, scruffy shoulder length

brown hair that could do with a wash. His month-old beard needs attention. It looks as though a pigeon has deposited its nesting materials then thought better of the housing. He's wearing brown Timberland boots and a blue check shirt. The description is purely for me to rehearse my observational recording, you can forget it.

He hands me a file marked 'Unident A'. It's thin. It contains a surveillance image of Miss Stone and Hamer getting into a black taxi outside arrivals at Heathrow. There's nothing else. Hudson looks up. An apologetic smirk on his face. "We need all you can get. A full profile."

"Leave it with me." I hand him back the file.

"You'll need the image. You need to know what she looks like!"

I tap my head. "It's all up here."

He shakes his head in disgust.

I take this as a perfect opportunity to leave. I collect my phones from the locker and slip the SIM cards back in. The Nokia breathes and I can relax. I smell her before I see her. The DCI is behind me; a fresh application of perfume has been applied.

"Here's my number. I want to know when you're out on my job. Every time. Not just when you feel like it. I don't imagine you'll be needing a desk here?"

I'm looking at my phone then turn to her. "No. You'll be the first to know when I have anything. Let me know when the next office meeting is and I'll be there."

"I look forward to seeing the results."

She turns and goes back into her domain. I show myself out. I know where I'm going and need the fresh air. I head towards the Thames. I come under the railway arch opposite Tintagel house. I stop to admire the graffiti, a Banksy-style image of a guy reaching for a love heart. It's positioned as though he's using a pipe attached to the wall to stand up and reach it. Clever, even though it's crime, I admire the ingenuity and thought that has gone into its execution.

It's not all about the picture. The location is key to make

the art work. I come out and head towards the MI6building. Its masts and radars protrude from the roof. The cameras sweep the area. You can have all the technology in the world but nothing beats face-to-face combat when it comes to accessing criminals. I get the underground from Vauxhall to Brixton. Change at the end of the line and come back. My thoughts are drawn to Hamer; he's a busy man. I'd met him two weeks earlier in a hotel in Bali.

On surfacing I'm happy I'm alone. I grab a bus and go home.

Initial meeting with UCO went as expected. He is a jumped-up over-opinionated prick. Just within the age range of my target's associates but without the same degree of flair.

He looks as though his life has been one long Caribbean holiday. He clearly keeps fit but I would surmise this is for appearances rather than sport.

I have no idea as to his experience in the field and his personnel file is poor. From initial looks it would appear to have been redacted leaving only the bare minimum of papers. I would have expected more with his level of service.

He has no respect of rank and is clearly under supervised. I am as satisfied as I can be that he will be monitored by his own unit whilst deployed.

He has been read his status and authority level by myself and signed to this effect. I have been given no opportunity to look at where his deployment would be useful and it would appear I won't be afforded it either. SCO35 have his control and the crossover with my investigation is a real shit.

He will have no direct access to my unit and only have a key card for the main door to the building to attend office meetings.

I asked him to sign a memorandum of understanding and inclusion notice, which he did.

I have noted my feelings as to his presence and use during this operation and can do no more at this stage. Should he interfere with my investigation I will make my views known and request his return to unit. I have also asked that he report regularly to me with any new intelligence and attend office meetings as directed.

I have provided him with my contact number and he is aware he can contact me 24/7.

I can only investigate Guardino with the limited resources I have. Issues of national security are not my remit and of little concern to me on this enquiry.

Initial briefing given and action accepted by DS Batford to target unidentified female, action 34 refers.

DS Hudson aware, on HOLMES desk.

The target is of little importance to me despite my enthusiasm in the briefing.

As I expected DS Batford can't resist a blonde with big tits and leapt at the chance to establish contact and ID female.

This should keep DS Batford out of the picture for a while leaving my team to concentrate on Guardino's driver and associates.

3

<u>Bali – June</u>

Ben Hamer is having a bad day. "What do you fucking mean you don't have a villa? I specifically booked a fucking villa with my own pool and complete fucking privacy."

His accent invades the serenity of the hotel reception area. I could see this was not the start to the holiday he'd expected.

The manager approaches him and motions to a side room, which he declines. "Look, can you fucking read?" Hamer flips open the titanium laptop cover and the screen illuminates. He clicks the mouse pad and a video plays the layout of the villa he had been expecting to accommodate. I have a good view from where I am.

"Sir, we have no villa available at the moment. We have an oil convention here and all villas are currently occupied. Please, let me show you to your room, it has a sea view and is spacious."

The manager pauses, hoping Hamer will concede. Hamer takes a deep breath.

"I am not taking no for a fucking answer. I spent an extra five hundred dollars specifically for the promised, FULL, Indonesian experience. Read it! This included my OWN, I repeat MY OWN fully enclosed private fucking villa with personal attendant. Now go fix it."

He shuts the lid to his Apple Mac Pro and walks to a

seated area in the lobby. "Hey, I'll be over here. I expect you back with my key and a bag boy in five." Hamer enforces the time requirement by showing the manager his limited-edition Rolex watch and tapping the watch face. Hamer has ten days to indulge with the lady of his choice. She joins him after inspecting the bathroom, applying makeup and tying up her recently dyed blonde hair. He pats the seat beside him. She sits down and stares at her nails in admiration. Hamer stretches out his legs and checks his watch. The manager has two more minutes.

Two minutes pass. I've been monitoring the wall clock whilst appearing to polish the reception counter. He would be your average hostage taker's worst nightmare. You'd throw in the towel after thirty minutes and give yourself up putting it down to a bad day at the office.

"Well? I don't see any key or bag boy. I would advise you NOT to fuck with me. If I don't get the villa I booked I swear I will just make my way to the first one I see and take it. Do you understand the gravity of this situation? Who else can I speak to? I have no faith that you even understand what I'm saying. Get me someone above you, now!"

Hamer moves around the desk and bangs on a staff door. Other staff begin ushering guests towards the cocktail bar whilst Hamer continues his assault on the Balinese oak.

I hear the whole conversation. That's what happens when you're assigned to front desk area. I'd requested the duty. I already knew Hamer was arriving today. I also knew that I would be his personal attendant. I knew how to alter the booking system to make it appear as though there was no spare villa. Why would I do this? I need to be his saviour, because I'd been told to look after him and give him everything he was entitled to. It was my brief. It was my job and I'd spent the last two months awaiting his arrival. Like his watch, it was precision engineered. My firm knew he was in trouble. The tap on an associate's phone confirmed it.

Hamer's boss was getting nervous around the chain of tanning shops laundering his drug money. The shops were becoming popular, not just for the leather skins wanting to top up but from other firms wanting to cash in on his enterprise. Now these 'firms' won't go and get a business loan from a high street bank, oh no. These firms just move in. A business takeover if you will, but without the paperwork. That's why he's under pressure. My people knew he would be sent here, as this place was Vincenzo's favourite destination. He'd invested money in The Reef. So the police took a gamble and got me out here to get a job and be in place for his arrival. Hamer had another job. Come up with an alternative cash flow plan to run alongside the salons or retire. Hamer was onto a good thing.

He wasn't about to throw in the towel and open a pretzel franchise. His idea of addressing the issue was to start talking to police. Hamer wanted out. What Hamer didn't know is that the police weren't interested in dodgy tax affairs. They wanted the whole empire. What the old bill didn't bank on was Hamer going sour over his cut of the cash from the information he provided. We have many bills to pay on a reduced government payroll. Informants are way down the list of cash recipients, especially the two million he was hoping to get.

So how does he resolve the issue? He begins channelling funds away from the salons and into an Albanian car wash he set-up and oversaw. It was good business. I mean, 200 cars a day and a £20,000 per week turnover has to be, doesn't it? The thing is, Hamer's time was running out. I know this because I'm here and the job needs putting to bed. My role? Get close to Hamer and find out Big H's next move. Big H is Vincenzo Guardino the largest importer of heroin in Europe. Hamer is an arsehole.

I wait. Never rush. I learnt the worst you can do is intervene early when a guy is getting heated and smashing his fists into an inanimate object. In a bullfight the matador waits for the animal to tire before he goes for the kill. It can get tedious seeing another human being in such distress even for a voyeur of human nature. I approach the desk and speak with Robert, the services manager.

"Finally you've some fucking sense. I take it this is the bag boy?" Hamer points at me. I don't react. It isn't my place. We're not formally introduced and my role hasn't been explained. The manager takes over. "Mr Hamer, sir. I am very happy to tell you that we do have a villa prepared for you and your companion. This is Mr Sky and he will be your assistant for the duration of your stay here. Mr Sky has personally requested this role and I am happy for him to undertake it. Please come and find me or send Mr Sky should anything not be to your satisfaction, sir."

The manager bows his head and places his hands as if in prayer. I do the same but unlike the manager I don't let my eyes leave Hamer as I bow.

"Well hoo fucking rah. Take my bags and be careful with them. Get me to my villa and I hope to God it's the one I booked on your website." Hamer summons his lady. His bags are crammed in the seated area by her feet. Each one of the five-piece Louis Vuitton luggage set looks new, never before travelled. I can tell a traveller's luggage set having worked at The Reef for the last two months. I have a luggage cage so this would be no problem. I couldn't help but wonder what contents were in his lady's case. Sex toys, no doubt, for her not him. No way he could satisfy her, he has no patience.

I'd seen it all here. Most couples are discreet the first week then they just accept me as one of the family, well, slave, and couldn't give a shit what they leave out for me to clear away. For the record I don't swear in front of guests or monks, but in my head, well that's game on. I mention monks as I live within a Buddhist community when I leave the hotel. Why? I teach them English. In return I get to stay in a single-room Indonesian wooden hut on a raised platform. I still claim hotel room rate expenses from the police. I work in one after all.

I have a bed mat, a small desk and a carved wooden Buddha statue. All my washing, which is minimal, I get done by the hotel laundry in exchange for medication I acquire from the guests.

This isn't stealing. It's doing the laundry staff a service to prevent sickness by medication they can't access or afford. I make my way to the villa with Hamer and his woman behind me, following like I own them. I check the key number against the villa gate that encloses their private garden, pool and beach. I knew it was this one but thought the delay would add to their 'Indonesian experience'.

"This better be the one, bag boy."

I turn the key, open the door and invite them in to their own private paradise. He goes in first, followed by the blonde who has looked up from her hands and nails and is taking in the scene. Wooden loungers with luxuriant mattresses guard the private pool. The bougainvillea petals rest on the water. I spend half my time fishing these out whilst spreading virgin petals on the bed to add to the romantic feel. Wind chimes add to the ambience with a soothing lament. Statues of lions add a certain regal and opulent quality to the courtyard and outside dining area.

"You can put the bags inside the room."

I do as he asks, making sure the bags are secure. I wheel the cart back to the pool area. Hamer's sitting on a lounger checking his shades; she's on her phone.

"Hey! What did I tell you about no phones here? Are you fucking thick? Give it here." She comes off the phone and hands it to him.

"Who was it?" he demands.

"It was the cattery telling me Oscar was okay," she almost whimpers, losing her air of confidence. He says nothing as she leaves, tears forming, heading into the villa. I wait as she passes.

"Hey. Don't just stand there. The show's over and there's no tip. Where do I get a drink?" I stop the cart.

"Mr Hamer, sir. If you will allow me to take this cart back I will return and fix whatever drink you wish." It's in my job description.

"Oh yeah? What part of 'there's no tip' don't you fucking get?" He raises both hands in front of him.

"Sir, I expect nothing in return. It's my job to assist you whilst you stay with us. I am your attendant at this villa and require no further payment."

He looks confused for a second then begins nodding in recognition of my role as slave.

"Right…right, now I get it. You're a little old to be a bag boy so I guess they keep you on out of sympathy. Get rid of the cart then come back in and unpack our stuff and mix me a scotch on the rocks, no water." He leaves and so do I.

It's calm outside Villa Trauma. Guests mingle in the lobby waiting for taxis to take them outside for the evening. Why you'd want to leave here is anyone's guess. You have a choice of five exquisite restaurants catering for every taste that provides a good rotational dining experience for the duration of your stay. I figured Hamer and his woman would need some space to clear the air so I go and see Sinta in laundry.

Sinta means chastity. In Sinta's case this is not adhered to. She runs the 'pharmacy' amongst the community as well as other personal services. She's in her early twenties but inhabits a body of advanced years. This doesn't seem to damage her trade. I'm at an advantage in the pharmaceutical sense as I'd seen Blondie's nose and she's bang on cocaine for sure. She will have a prescribed substitute in case of drought and that will be good for Sinta and good for me. I know the signs of drug misuse. Every good attendant should. It provides security for you and the guest in the event of accusations or drug withdrawal.

The kind of drugs I'm hoping Blondie will have: Baclofen, Disulfiram, Modafini or Propranolol. I don't mention this to Sinta. She has my laundry and I don't want to let her down. I figured they'd had long enough back at the villa and a runner I'd sent confirmed he had seen them walking about their private garden.

On my way back I go via the lobby, log into Hamer's

room account and add a $300 bottle of Highland Park twenty-five-year-old single malt whisky. He will settle the account at the end and won't quibble. I also feel like a treat. I go to the wine and spirits vault and speak to Anak.

Anak isn't like Sinta. Anak is around fifty-five, wears small round spectacles and walks with a slight stoop from working in the vault for so long. If it's not a verifiable order, then no booze. That's why the management put him in there. He checks the screen, sees the approved entry and smiles a satisfied smile to himself as he disappears. He returns, carrying an oak box with the ornate Celtic symbol of the brewer that he opens to reveal the bottle, which is as it should be. He nods. I take the case and he bows. I sign, bow, leave and head back.

I arrive to a calmer reception. Hamer is inside, jet-lagged and asleep. Blondie is poolside on a lounger in a two-piece Paul Smith bikini, a floral design befitting the setting.

I don't approach her. If she wants something she can summon me. At the edge of the pool is the private bar they can swim up to and sit at whilst drinking. It is also a small haven for wasps that gather to enjoy any sweet leftovers. My time here hasn't been wasted. I devised a feeding bowl the wasps would congregate at, feed and go fully satiated. It also adds credence to my cover story.

A small crowd gathers as a fresh dish of nectar in the form of Pepsi is placed out. I had just started cutting some fresh coconut when I see Blondie's hand go up to her head in a salute to shield her eyes. Her other hand waves me over.

I hope she's applied lotion. I hate getting my hands sticky whilst dressed.

"Hi, I wanna drink?"

Her accent is North London, more Islington than Muswell Hill.

"What drink would you like, Miss…?"

"Stone. Zara Stone. A rum and Coke, ta."

"Ice? Miss Stone."

"Go on then."

"You don't sound like the others here."

The others. That could mean any number of nationalities that are at the hotel but I surmise she means the staff.

I dismiss the question.

"May I ask where you have travelled from, Miss Stone?"

"Hackney, London. Do you know London?"

"I have visited once or twice. A charming city."

I wasn't far off in my estimation as to location. If I were to be pedantic the boundaries overlap.

"Charming? It's a fucking shithole. You never visited Hackney then, that's for sure."

I bow and go and prepare her drink. She lays back down on her back with her hands now stretched out behind her head. From my view at the bar I can tell her tits are fake. Her belly button's pierced. Underneath it is a tattoo of a lotus flower. Its open petals cradle the gem. It all looks cheap, apart from the tits. Tits like those have Harley Street credentials. If I were to look properly they're probably trademarked.

She's around six foot tall. Hamer looks like a midget against her but small enough for him to feel empowered. After all, he's an accountant and wants to protect his investment. That means paying $650 for a bikini with a made-to-measure top. I have no idea how she came to know him, but that can wait.

I add the obligatory straw, cocktail umbrella and carry the drink on a small silver tray, napkin supplied.

"You can put it down there, ta."

I had guessed the table next to the lounger was a safe option.

She takes a sip and looks at me over the top of her Armani sunglasses, leaning on her elbows.

"So…how long have you been here then?"

"Long enough. I enjoy the sea and of course making sure guests have a pleasant stay."

I lie, but I've perfected the art of appearing sincere. Her accent stabs at my skull dragging up memories of tougher times. No wonder she never spoke outside the villa, Hamer would never permit that.

There's still no sign of Hamer emerging from their love pit. I made sure that he could see us when he woke up.

I seize this early opportunity

"Do you enjoy London?"

"I live on an estate run by gangs. It ain't all that but it's all I've ever known." I nod in recognition, indicating I'm listening.

"How did you meet Mr Hamer?"

She hesitates and takes a sip of her drink.

"He met me at a strip club in Green Lanes and liked what he saw. Said he'd show me a good time and offered to look after me. He's an arrogant prick but he's loaded, so game on I say."

She carries on drinking and begins to relax. Her secret's out and she can be herself. I find this honesty endearing, if not a little naive. I also know that as soon as he wakes she'll act differently towards me. That's what's expected when you are 'just staff'.

This is one subject I have the most difficulty accepting. Take a large burger chain or restaurant; do you think those that serve you are uneducated or lazy? No. The majority, are university educated and intelligent. All waiting for work, in their trained fields, to arise. In the meantime there are still bills to pay. To be of service is the most honourable of trades.

Hamer slept four hours. I sweep the patio and drag leaves from the surface of the pool. Every now and then a painted bronzeback tree snake appears. I make a note of where it is just in case it decides to move down its perch. I know they're harmless, but guests don't like sharing their habitats and get as skittish as an untrained racehorse on seeing one. The sun greets us with temperate arms but at this early hour of the day it seeks nothing more. Miss Stone is happy with her drink.

I take advantage of the impasse to place a banana leaf

basket of flowers and fruit on the small courtyard shrine and light an incense stick. This is for my benefit, keeping me focused on my job and patient in my role. One thing my training taught me was to spend time getting in role. Here I'm not a copper, I'm a servant to the rich. It's imperative I remain so. Goffman was a shrink who had a vision he called a dramaturgical theory. We all have different masks. We choose one to wear dependant on the situation and others' expectation of it.

"Hey Fly, or whatever your name is. Come over here and fix me a drink like I asked. And let me set some ground rules for our stay here."

The fat bastard is awake.

I don't react immediately, bow to the shrine then begin walking towards my entertainment for the week. I know it's for a week even though they are booked for ten days. This was going better than expected. As I approach he's sitting on the edge of the deck, the white linen robe his only comfort. His gut crease appears above the tie line. His gold neck chain buries into his grey chest hair. If he were to sit naked his tits and stomach would replicate the face of Homer Simpson. I bow to him.

"I hope you slept well Mr Hamer. I took the liberty of providing this twenty-five-year-old scotch. I am sure it will meet with your approval." I get the bottle out of the oak case and make him a drink. I couldn't give a shit whether he likes it or not. For all I care my own piss would be too good for him, warm or with ice. I hand him the crystal glass and he looks at it suspiciously before tasting. The nod of approval takes an age and I stand, as is customary, awaiting further direction.

"Great choice, for a bag boy. Here's what I expect out of this deal. I want you here when I need you and not when you see fit to show up. Second. See her? That girl is off limits to your mind and your kind. Touch her and I won't be responsible for my actions – and third, sort out the bathroom. I took a shit and backed it up. That's all."

Hamer turns away and indicates he requires the large Cuban lighting that's rammed in his fat lips. This is the attitude I referred to earlier.

I pull on some gloves from the cleaning store, which is a hut discreetly hidden amongst trees a good distance from the dwelling. The bathroom is a generous size and decorated luxuriously with Indonesian stone tiles and gold taps on the his and hers sinks. No amount of luxury will solve the drainage and sewerage problem.

I kneel down by the toilet, turn away and stick my gloved hand down into the U-bend. There's a sound of gurgling as trapped air releases, along with the foul smelling stench of Hamer's deposit. His roughage is good. I extract a solid stool. I place this in a bucket, wipe up and spray some perfume. Hamer is still where I left him, his cigar dying with his every breath. I go around the back of the villa with my bucket of shit. It would be sanitary to dispose of this in a main bin but they had already been collected.

Under the villa is a crawl space. The design allows for air to circulate and the heat of the sand to provide an ambient floor temperature. You can't have guests suffering cold feet. I take off my whites, check around, open the hatch and crawl in, taking the bucket. I know where the bedroom is. I'm also aware how the heat of the sand will generate sufficient warmth to remind him of the gift he'd left me.

Operation Filth, done. I crawl back out, dust the sand from my body and put my whites back on. In a day, maybe two, he will bring up the smell and I will contact a non-existent villa engineer. Over the years I've found if you treat people with respect you get it back. This applies whatever your line of business or whoever you choose to associate with and call friends. Personally I have no time for friendship. An attachment disorder, a psychologist told me.

Hamer has his eye on the prize and dismisses me, taking Miss Stoner, as I now like to call her, back into the villa. I go to my equipment hut, change into a T-shirt, linen trousers and trainers for the journey home. Nothing better than feeling the earth beneath your feet as you burn off the tension of being treated like a subservient all day by a pompous prick of a Yank. Each step feels good. I exit the hotel, waving to the guard on the gate, and leave opulence for reality.

Bali is Nirvana. It has everything I could want. Indigenous people, who don't ask personal questions. Beautiful climate. Relaxed attitude to dogs. I would be joined by the odd dog on my walks home and knew they relished the freedom as much as me. Nusa Dua is where I've lived for the past two months. I had to fit in and get the hotel job. It was a risk but a calculated one. Having a foreigner is good for business. It's the rainy season now. The tourists still arrive on cheaper package deals. I take a good lungful of air as I connect to sand and dust. I follow the road that leads up to the monastery and my humble dwelling. There are a hundred monks living in the grounds, worshipping in the temple. You would never know by their absence. That is until a glut of rehab pawns enter the monastery gates.

The West call it rehab, the monks call it awakening. Cleansing the mind and body of all impurities. Back home, people like to partake of these experiences in a setting within a health and safety conscious environment, staffed by trained drug and alcohol counsellors with the visiting alternative therapist thrown in for good measure.

The monks see it differently. They take no prisoners. The druggies are free to leave if they wish but they don't have the energy to. Forced vomiting to expel the toxins is a favourite. Legal waterboarding. A necessary evil. All walks of life convey on this haven. Each one a train wreck from start to finish. The wailing is the worst as they come off whatever drug of choice they've been imbibing. I was used to seeing the prone shaking bodies that couldn't make it from the floor to their blanket. Walking meditation was a regular sight. A diatribe of abuse would spew forth from the zombie line. The monks just ignored it. Did I feel pity? No. Why should I? We all make choices, I've made mine, and they've made theirs.

A junior monk bows, opens the wooden doors that lead out onto the main courtyard. I stop, bow, and then enter. I look up at the temple. A number of monks are sweeping the many steps that lead to the entrance. To the left of the courtyard is a path. I walk towards it, sweat pouring off me, and make my way past chickens and goats to my hut. There's no one to greet me, only the space I had left.

My home is raised five feet from the floor on a wooden frame. This helps when it rains heavily. It also stops snakes and other ground-dwelling creatures from choosing your pad as their home of choice. The roof is made from bamboo, bound together with string to create a watertight environment. It's small. The entire floor space is ten foot by ten foot. The only contents are my mattress, blanket and a small table for me to read or write at.

I have no power, only candles. I have a window. A wooden frame, no glass with shutters on the outside. When closed they form the Coca Cola logo. My clothing is limited. No wardrobe required.

My only storage is a locked metal box three foot by two foot that I've buried under the footings of my hut, the contents of which I don't require right now.

I go to the communal wash area and clean up before I get dressed. I don't use the soap here; I use the hotel's. The water tank is full since the last downpour of rain but I only stay under enough to feel the moisture erode my sweat. I feel like a fraud, residing here. The monks need the wash water more than me. At the stainless steel wash stands I look up into a grimy mirror. I shave my head and face. My skin is sensitive today. My shaved head now used to the sun. As I towel dry the sun fades and bids me goodnight.

I knew Hamer was out this evening as I'd organised his transport. He hadn't said where he was going but I'd supplied the sat nav and would return the hired Jeep. That would give me all I needed to know. I get out of the monastery and onto the main road, walk to a nearby taxi hut.

A cab is available. I get in. I need a break. Reflect and gather my thoughts. Plan my next move.

Indonesian chatter invades the cab's speaker. My native driver attempts to switch channels on the radio, one eye on the wheel the other on the road. The single track stretches out in front, bathed only in moonlight. The dim headlights fight with the dust and stone for recognition, hunting like a camera lens with no contrast to focus on. It had been an arid day. I ask the driver to turn up the air-con, which he reluctantly does. He's clearly of the school that cool air wastes fuel. I surmise this from the vast sweat patch that his white cotton shirt has absorbed against the tan leather seat. I settle back and gaze out the window at the passing darkness, trying in vain to dump my thoughts at the roadside.

My mind's distracted by the intrusion of oncoming headlights. My driver finds a Cuban radio station and taps out a samba rhythm on his steering wheel. The vehicle slows. I move to the middle seat as the cab's front beam illuminates a cluster of red and yellow lights in the distance. I tell my driver to kill ours and go off road. He does. No cab driver wants to get involved in another motorist's drama. Time is money. We get close enough not to be noticed, but far enough away for me to use a night sight I'd taken from my buried crate.

I'd recognise a Jeep's taillights anywhere. I put the scope to my right eye and adjust the focus. The night turns green and the vehicle lights flicker iridescently. It's not the only thing that's illuminated. A pool of fluid becomes a sea of dark mass in the lens. I've seen this before, it's blood, lots of it. I can make out a head buried into the road's surface, an arm outstretched in a vain attempt to clutch at life. The Jeep's tyres have picked up the blood. The road's become its canvas ending in a swirling stop. What I assume was a male is clearly dead. I come to this conclusion as the head's detached from the body, as is the arm.

Hamer is absent. I know it's their Jeep from the registration. I can make out a cycle at the roadside and also

Stoner. She is freaking out, walking in circles, no shoes on. Both front doors to the Jeep are open. Hamer has done a runner. I tell the driver to wait. He agrees and asks no more. He also knows I pay well. I get out and move slowly towards the Jeep, keeping low, using coarse scrub as cover. Another set of headlights approaches. I have to be quick. I run across the road to the rear of the Jeep and set down in a crouch at the back. Stoner can't see me. I wait until she moves towards the side of the Jeep then grab her by the mouth and drag her into the scrub. The approaching lights slow. The scene turns macabre as the headlights scan it. The pedal bike is a mangled mess. The rider's head is now an integral part of the road, as is his arm. The rest of his body has been flung on impact and is nowhere obvious.

The car doesn't stop. The driver has seen enough, wants no involvement. The car's back wheel reinforces the skull's burial. I slowly release my hand from her mouth as I whisper in her ear that it's me and not to shout.

"Fuckin hell, fuckin hell. That Yank cunt just fucked off leaving me here to take the rap." She's sobbing now, leaning into me.

"What am I going to do? They'll hang me here if they think it was me. I ain't no grass. I can't tell anyone it was him driving. I told the stupid bastard he was off his head to drive but he just wouldn't listen. You've got to get me out of this."

She's looking at me now, I can tell, even in our dark shroud, as her breath is close to my face. I'm not surprised at how the rich desert the poor. Hamer is naive to think the police won't want to speak to the hirer of the car. Stoner is guilty by association and I need this as leverage.

I work quickly, clearing the car of debris that could contain fingerprints or DNA. I tell her to grab the sat nav. I say I worked quick; she did all the work. I touch nothing. I don't even go near the Jeep's interior. She puts the spent bottle of Jack Daniels in her bag and recovers her shoes.

I take her back to the cab. We get in and go back to The Reef hotel. The hotel's not that busy. It's around 0100 hours.

Staff change over. I take her through the gardens and into her villa. She's shaking, makeup running down her cheeks. I fix her a drink and tell her to wait and speak to no one.

"Don't go, please don't go. He'll be fucking livid when he gets back. If he gets back." I sit down on the king-size bed I'd made that morning. She's sitting alongside me, head in her hands, cleavage showing through the low-cut blue satin dress she is wearing. Her blonde hair over her hands, poker straight despite the night's trauma. Her nails remain pristine. It would be so easy to take advantage of the situation but I remain professional.

"If he comes back and touches you I'll deal with it. Wait here. Back in five." I leave her sitting on the bed. I go to the equipment shed and get a tin marked with the hazardous substance symbol. I open it and take out the mobile phone from inside. I'd made sure it had a full battery before their arrival. I power it up and the SIM shows it's operative. This is a risk but one I must take. Hamer is not a fan of phones on this trip. I go back into the villa. Miss Stoner is in the shower. Her dress lies on the floor along with her thong. I pick up the hotel phone and dial reception.

It's answered on the second ring. "It's Sky, Villa Hamer. Phone the police and report the Hamer rental Jeep stolen. It was taken five hours ago."

I hang up. The risk is minimal. Vehicles get stolen all the time here, especially rentals. I'd arranged for it to be parked away from the hotel. There will be no CCTV. The way I figured it, they were here for another nine days, the investigation won't even get off the ground whilst they are here. As for the head in the road, he wouldn't be the first pissed cyclist to be collected by a drug-fuelled tourist on his way to who knows where. I see the sat nav in her shoulder bag and retrieve it. I open the side window and throw it out onto the garden for collection later.

Enter Hamer. He announces his arrival by hammering on the villa gate. I'd purposefully locked it in the event that my professionalism waned and Stoner succumbed. Stoner has heard his announcement on the door and is now out of the shower wrapped in a towel. I have to be quick. "Here take this phone and keep it out of sight. My number is in it. Just call if you need to." She nods in recognition of the gesture and the need to keep it discreet. She goes into the kitchen and finds a pan drawer and places it in there. The fat bastard enjoys food but will never cook it.

I compose myself and go out to the garden gate. The banging is now causing residents to wake and security won't be far off. I open the door just as he's about to bang his fist again, and catch his ring-bedecked infested hand in mine. I maintain the pressure as he comes through. I let go and lock the door. He's pissed. He can barely stand, let alone speak. A fortunate state to be in. I help him up into the villa and lay him on the couch. He's saying nothing coherent. He mutters, letting strings of saliva careen down his chins and settle in his neck creases.

My energy is draining. Mental tension along with the physical exertion of dragging a beached whale to his bed has taken its toll. I throw a blanket over him. He's out of it. Stoner is now in her nightwear. She comes over and we step out into the garden.

"He's gone for the foreseeable. The police won't come tonight; they'll be here tomorrow. Tell them you went to find the car at eight p.m. and it was gone. The car was meant to be unlocked and the key in the glove box. Tell me you understand what you have to say."

She repeats it back. "How did you know what to do tonight?"

She's lit up a fag and offers me one. I take it. I look back at Hamer. No change.

"I used to be into this and that. I'm not proud of my past, but that's all behind me now. You learn, remember what you need and what you don't."

She looks at me and blows a plume of smoke into the pure Bali air.

"I knew you weren't right for here. What you here for

really? Who are you running from?"

I light up my cigarette and take a lungful. "I don't know what you mean. I found religion and now I'm travelling and teaching English where I can, picking up bits of work every now and then."

"I don't know no religion where the God has produced a mobile phone out of nothing."

She smiles coyly. I don't answer immediately. I need time to think through my next step. She's comfortable having me here. That already shows. But it's not about now; it's about the future. I don't need her now. I need her for the next three weeks. I realise this is my only shot. There will be no other moment.

"Ok. As you're so interested and unlikely to see me again once you leave. I used to drive lorries. I was taken on by a guy, for a special delivery. He needed some tools, you know, guns. I knew an army guy who'd come back from Afghanistan. He had some 9mm Glock pistols he needed to offload. They got together and a deal was struck. I was to take them from a lockup in Kent over to Ireland where money had already been exchanged. There was to be a meet at the lockup by my man and this other guy to make sure the goods got on my wagon. As I turn up, they're getting the crates out. Next minute the old bill had shooters at their heads and shouting blue murder. I do the honourable thing. Reverse and fuck off." I stare out beyond the pool and watch a lizard run up the garden wall. Blondie lights up another cigarette. I get up, fix us both a drink. Hamer reminds us of his condition through his open mouth.

"Do you still do that kind of stuff or 'ave you given up?"

"Never asked again, to be honest. I will have to go back soon though. My old man's on his last legs. I've got enough money to get back. There's not much call for the likes of me back home for work. I mean who wants a bald headed guy who's found religion?"

I sip Hamer's Scotch and savour the moment. It's all we have and I intend to milk this one. I wait. I've thrown out the bait. See, Hamer is small fry. Miss Stone is the prize. The one with the links. You don't get flown out on a jolly. Not in this game. The police want value for money. Hamer didn't choose Miss Stoner for company. She attached herself to him. Blondie is Guardino's star attraction and closest confidante. She will also put out at a cost.

London was too close for this kind of recruitment. It had to work, whatever the cost.

"What's with the name, Sky? Sounds a bit queer if you ask me." A plume of smoke fills my face as she asks.

"I was named after the ward I was left on. Apparently my mother presented at the hospital, gave birth to me and fucked off. It was the maternity wing's opening day. I was the first born on it." She says nothing. How can you respond other than with trite pacifying noises? It was a lie anyway. There had been a boy by the name of Sky Riley born. He'd died at birth and I'd taken on his identity. It wasn't common practice anymore to use the identities of dead children but I'd ignored that direction. I wanted to give him a life he'd never had. Doing something worthwhile. I would visit his grave on his birthday but leave nothing. The greatest gift I could give him was my legacy.

I feel a hand on my knee. I don't turn. Just look ahead. There's a bond between fostered children. Even if one party is unaware of the other's history.

"I've got your number. I know a man who's looking for a driver, as it goes. It'll pay well and if you get on then there's loads more work."

"Well, you've got my number now, call me."

She winks at me and I raise my glass. My work here is done.

She's getting tired and I need to go. I resist asking about her past as I know it from social services records. It would be too easy to slip up with a fact I couldn't have known. I know I'll be leaving tomorrow morning. I've sown the seed for my exit strategy and it's come up early. I'm confident she'll call. Why? I saved her ass and she owes me and we have similar life experience, so she thinks. I know the police won't be bothered with the accident. After two months, I've learnt how they deal with these things. I also know Miss Stone will call Big H who will call Hamer. Hamer will be told to sort it. Money will be exchanged and the investigation will become an accident with an inconclusive end.

As for Zara Stone, she never commented on the money going over before the guns. That never happens and tells me Big H is careful in how he educates his business associates. Hamer has seen me briefly but not enough that he would have any positive recall of me. Even more so when I have hair. I leave and get into a hotel cab. The cab drops me at a twenty-four-hour supermarket and I use the public call box. I dial an international number and wait. I don't think about the time difference. I know it will be picked up. It rings four times and is answered.

"Yes"

"Sky. It's done. Book me a flight for eleven hundred hours my time. I'll collect the tickets at the airport desk."

The line goes dead. I replace the receiver and get back in the waiting cab. He knows I'm a good fare and is prepared to wait whilst I pack. He drops me at departures. On the journey I talk about how my father is gravely ill and I need to get back. He'll feed that back to the hotel and that will get to Stoner via Sinta who will be looking to offload my laundry to the next bell boy servicing their villa. My belongings are all in a rucksack, the contents of the crate, including passport and cash. The night sight I've dumped. It's been a long wait. I need to get home.

4

This is one of the things I love. Waiting for the prey to enter my territory, then stalking it until I pounce. I don't kill. I collect.

It's 1900 hours. I'm in a restaurant looking out of the window at Mount Pleasant Sorting Office. Watching North Londoners busying themselves on their routes from work to home or work to pub. Miss Stoner is late. I order a coffee, pay my debt and wait. The waiter offers me a receipt. I decline. Receipts are a record of where you go or have been. Cops hang on to them to claim expenses. Pockets are for hands, nothing else. I will always get expenses back. I'm never out of cash.

1910 hours. The coffee is tepid. I glance down at my phone on the table. The screen is blank. I look out and see the black cab, the one that was in the photo DS Hudson showed me, pull up opposite the post office. Stoner gets out. Doesn't pay and the cab drives off towards Holborn. She's alone. She takes out her phone and my screen lights up and the table vibrates. I keep looking before answering.

"Alright. I'm here. Where are you? It's fuckin' starting to rain."

Small droplets appear at my window providing good cover from the street looking in. I remain seated.

"See the phone box to your left." She turns.

"Yeah. What about it?"

"Go in there and wait."

"You're fuckin' weird. I'm only doing it because it's pissing it down. Hurry up. Hang on…how do you know where I am?"

I hang up.

I watch her go in. The collar on her three-quarter-length Marc Jacobs coat is up. She still has a good tan. I was hoping she'd be casually dressed. I grab my jacket and leave. This is a time that I feel most on edge. The moment before meeting. Not knowing who could be watching the watcher. I know the NCA team weren't out. They were all at a leaving drink in the city. The cab hadn't come back and wasn't parked up. Road works wouldn't permit it. A stag party is coming along Pentonville Road. I cross and tag on the back. They welcome me with drunken arms as we cross towards the telephone box. As we approach I break off and knock on the glass. She turns.

"Fuck off I'm trying to make a call."

She pauses then the recognition takes place. She comes out.

"Didn't recognise you without your white suit on." She kisses me on the cheek. We walk down towards Smithfield.

"You fucked off pretty sharpish. Was it something I said?" She's smiling.

"My old man passed on. Had to leave. I didn't get to him in time." She squeezes my hand.

"Sorry babes."

"How was your holiday?"

"Shit. He got the arse because he wasn't getting any. I told him I had the decorators in. We had to move villa because there was a stink of shit and no one could tell us why. The filth came around and I did what you said. Hamer paid them off."

"So it was alright then."

"Could've been worse, I s'pose. I got a massage each day and some sunbathing, whilst he got pissed. He knocked me about a couple of times, mind. Fat cunt can't run though."

I could see faint bruising on her neck. The upturned collar wasn't a fashion statement. It was hiding finger marks.

I know where we're going. A small pub tucked away off Smithfield Market. We go in, she finds a booth. I go to the bar and order drinks. For her, vodka cranberry. I get a Scotch, no ice. The pub's quiet but enough conversation to drown us out. I sit down and make sure I've got a view of the only entrance and exit. She has her back to the door and the frosted window means we won't be seen. I need assurance on our first meeting in London. I don't need any interruptions from her side or mine. Anonymity is our shield.

She brings out her phone, puts it on the table whilst she searches her handbag. I'm conscious of the phone. Is she recording? Is it set with location services on? Is she stupid enough to be on Facebook with her current location popping up to be liked or shared? She finds the lipstick she was looking for and reapplies.

"Hey, I'd prefer it if we turned phones off. Old habits die hard."

She doesn't question and adheres to the request.

"Great to see you again. I didn't think I would." Best opening line I could come up with.

"I keep my word when someone looks out for me. Even a stranger. I know if you were still out there I wouldn't have taken a beating. But I understand why you had to leave."

"I'm glad you understand. Have you seen him since? Hamer?"

"Oh yeah, I haven't left his side much since we got back. It's not love or anything, it's more of a business arrangement."

"Business?"

She looks about before she continues. A trait that warms my heart.

"I do have a fella. He's the one I told you about that's looking for a driver. He's a fucker, an' all, but we get on alright. He never knocks me about unless I deserve it. He's Hamer's boss. Hamer looks after his cash flow. He should be making sure it's flowing in a positive direction. Recently he's been shoddy. Had his fingers in the till. I was sent to see if he spilled. Whilst we was out there other enquiries were being made into his lifestyle. Anyway, enough about me what about you? I thought you'd found religion, so what's with the Scotch?"

Cute. Clearly not the typical villain's bird. She's observant. Has a memory for detail. Something I'm glad to be aware of early doors.

"I had nothing when I was out there. The monastery put me up in return for me teaching English. I liked the lifestyle. No ties, no baggage. It runs out though. Life takes over. You can't run from responsibility. In the end you have to face the music."

I leave her with that and go back to the bar. The pub is fuller, which is a good thing. I watch her. She seems so young to have been caught up in violence and shit. She's only thirty-two and being pimped around blokes like Hamer. The Hugh Hefners of pond life. Still it's not my job to babysit the snout. It's my job to infiltrate her lover's firm. I return, drinks in hand. She looks up from her nails.

"I haven't got long. His lordship's driver will be back for me in about twenty minutes. I told him I was makeup shopping."

"Hamer uses a cab?"

"Nah, not him. My fella, Big H. It suits him. He can go anywhere and if he's ever asked, he's taking a cab. Ron is his driver. A big lump but handy with his fists and a toy if the heat's up."

I say nothing. I now know his transport, chauffeur, chauffeur's name and that he carries a gun every now and then.

"So what's this job?" It would be rude not to ask.

She leans in closer. Close enough for me to smell the last cigarette she had but not enough to feel like I should grab her head and stick my tongue down her throat.

"He wants to reference you before he makes a decision.

He has a different method though. He has a job for you and if it comes off then he'll consider taking you on."

She sits back and waits to see how I react. It's times like these you have to be careful not to appear too keen. Keenness can come across as desperation. I'm not desperate but I don't want to appear available for hire at any rate. Only a novice or street-level dealer would make that mistake.

"Well, that's mighty generous of a man I've never met. I'm no Johnny-fly-by-night, someone he can try and fit up with gear. Now I'm not saying fuck off, but I need to know what the job is he wants me to do and what the prize will be at the end for doing it. You know I need cash. I'm not looking for one hit of Charlie. I've got funeral bills to pay and people looking for me. I need to make hay then go back to my previous life of sun, sea and education."

She smiles. She knew I wasn't about to jump all over the first offer that came along. But she does know, or at least thinks she knows, I like her. How do I know that? Her tits are on show in a low-cut Nicole Farhi top and her pupils are as large as the bulge in my pants. Aside from that, she called me. Met me discreetly and is prepared to lie to Big H and Da Do Ron Ron.

I also know she has fifteen minutes left of her twenty to report back positive news and avoid a fist from the big man.

"You'll never meet him. That's not the way he works. You will see me again, and me only, until you're on the job. The first job is simple. I've a number and you need to call it and pick up a parcel and take it to the location you'll be given on collection. If you decide against it then it's been nice knowing you lover."

I finish my drink and she does the same. "Give me the number." She hands me a SIM card. "Ask for Ghost. He knows this number and is expecting the call. He'll tell you where to go. Oh, you won't need anything bigger than a Mini for this job. Once you're done, call me."

She turns to go, I gently take her arm.

"My new number's in your coat pocket. Never text or

leave a message. Once you've called clear your call history. If I don't pick up I'll call back and ask for Sinta."

"Oh cheers. The name of that whore from the hotel who told me you left and wanted cash for your fuckin' laundry? You owe me a score. Your laundry ain't here, it's in the hotel bin."

She smiles, leaves the pub and I go back to the bar and order another Scotch. I give her five minutes and leave. I have limited time. I need to get back to my digs.

5

By the time I get to Elephant and Castle the sun is setting. The sky appears blood red. I don't believe in omens. I don't have the luxury of time to sit on this job. Both my paymasters want results and quick. Every second gone is lost revenue. I find a call box. I dial in.

"Yes"

"It's Sky. I need a motor for tonight. Nothing flash but nothing shit. I have something. I'll leave details at the drop point. Leave the keys there in an hour."

"You alright?" My superintendent asks.

"Yeah, yeah, I'm good. All's good. I just need the keys and car. The details will be waiting for you."

I hang up. I go to a twenty-four-hour Tesco store and buy a pay as you go phone and car charger. I make my way home. It's good to be back in the sanctuary of my room. There's a retreat on in the Buddhist Centre. Everyone is in the main prayer room. The chanting is soothing. I got my room generously donated by the manager. I'd told him about my work abroad and the death of my father and that I was looking for work. He bought the story and agreed to put me up for a month. I intend to make a sizeable donation to their efforts to bring about peace and harmony. I don't drink or smoke. I plan. I scheme. I lie. Not the same three jewels the residents take refuge in.

I devour some leftover food the café has put out. I need my energy. Mentally and physically. Nerves are an occupational hazard. I've learnt to control them enough over the years but not to the point of complacency. I've changed into an old tracksuit. I put on a tattered baseball hat and shabby trainers. I don't look like a typical drug runner; more like a guy who needs to take a long look at his dress sense.

The streets are buzzing tonight. The air is warm. The night sky obscured by the animation of the city's lights. People are smiling. The city feels vibrant. I embrace this energy as I make my way to the gym. I nod to the new female on reception and show my card. She buzzes me in. I go to the locker room, unlock the padlock to locker 066. Inside is a padded envelope. I take it and leave another containing notes I'd made of today's meeting and my new number. I shut and lock the door. I put my parcel in my bag.

I grab a coffee and sit down in a quiet area of the gym cafe. I put the SIM in the phone I'd bought. There's enough battery for the call and I have the charger for the car. I'd already switched my old SIM over for Stoner's benefit and my bosses.

I check the time. It's 2230 hours. Time to make the call. The phone rings twice. A deep voice answers.

"Yo. Wassup?"

"Ghost?"

"The one and only."

"You have something for me."

"Damn right bruv. Where you at?"

"Just tell me where to meet."

"Get to The Emirates, by the cannon, then bell me again. Come on your own. If you ain't here by midnight then I'm thinkin' you're a fuckin' pumpkin and the deal's off."

The line goes dead. I get another coffee. I've no intention of turning up early to this party. The host is rude. Rudeness is unnecessary. The courier is like the fast food producer. He's your lifeline to feeling satiated. Don't fuck with the cook unless you want him to piss in your broth.

I open the envelope. There's a set of keys for a BMW 3 Series and a card attached with Danvers Street written on it.

There's also £1,000 in twenty-pound notes. I put the money in the bag and put the label in the bin and leave. Danvers Street is a mile away. I take advantage of my attire and exit the gym, moving at the best pace I can manage. In a war zone a soldier never leaves base slowly. You must move and weave. I keep a steady pace and cross footways regularly. You never upset traffic in your traverse. You must flow like mist.

I hit Danvers Street. There's no follow. A BMW 3 Series is parked on the nearside footway. I stop and tie my lace. No one is in the street. I click the fob and the vehicle's lights flick twice and the interior light stays off. Last thing I need is to be an illuminated target as I get in. I cross and enter driver's side flinging the bag into the passenger footwell. Key in. Ignition on and move off towards N7 and the Emirates Stadium. I have an hour.

The traffic is light over Blackfriars Bridge. The London Eye is lit for all to see. Red, white and blue tonight. As I pass Smithfield I think of the meeting earlier. I need this to work. Failure is not an option. My future depends on the outcome of this next meeting. The only thing I'm armed with is my wits.

I reach the agreed meet point with twenty minutes to spare. I park near Drayton Park tube and cut across the stadium concourse. I stop at the Gunners shop window and look in. I can see a set of garages opposite. Industrial not commercial. The unit's lights are on and a main gate shuts off the premises. Everywhere else is unlit. I can't get nearer to look. I figure my mystery voice is on the other side of the eight-foot double steel doors. I move off to a grassed area and make the call.

"Yo bruv. You here or what?"

"I'm here."

"You should be able to see some big fuck off doors bruv. Come over there and knock."

"I can see them."

I kill the line. Pull down my cap and walk over. A small

trickle of sweat forms and runs down my neck. I get a sense that this is it. My body already knows and is indicating its preparedness. I acknowledge it by tilting my head left and right, stretching my neck and shoulders. The gate has a camera to the upper left and I avoid looking into the lens. The lens moves down and I know they've seen me. They know I'm alone. There used to be backup in this job but those days have gone. I've chosen this path and it's up to me to keep it clear of debris.

I knock as directed and wait. I hear footsteps on the other side and a male's voice either talking to someone with them or on a phone. I hear the voice say they'd bell them later and the gate opens enough for me to move in. I've reached the other side. A black male greets me. Late thirties, tied back dreadlocked hair, small goatee and a wide smile. He's dressed in mechanics overalls and reeks of engine oil and hard graft.

"Alright bruv, come, come."

The main garage is under a railway arch. It houses one hydraulic ramp and a floor pit. Work benches either side. A black Range Rover Evoque with blacked out windows is in the air. A mechanic stops welding and lifts up his weld visor. He takes it off. He's a white guy, mid-forties, large build, hands like shovels. He puts his equipment down and comes over. Sweat runs down his face from his bald head. I remain steady. Only one entrance and exit. I can see no one else. I make the first move and walk towards a wooden workbench and lean against it. The bald heavy comes over.

"Quick pat down mate. You know how it is." I lift my arms up. He pats down my upper body checking my sides, neck and crotch.

"Take the top off."

I do as asked.

"Turn around."

"You seen enough?"

"Yeah. Nice ink."

On my back is an image of Jos A Smiths, Priest Of Dark

Flight. It depicts a dark priest with hands in prayer. An eagle above his head with wings expanded and looking directly at you. The priest is anything but saintly. He's clad in medieval armour. I choose to use part of my cover story.

"I had it done in Bali by a monk. He was fucked off doing the usual tribal and religious shit."

My top is now on and I've seen enough.

"Get mine in Chapel Market."

He lifts his T-shirt and his back has a tiger climbing up from the base of his spine to over his right shoulder. It's bold and fills his broad frame. It would have cost over a grand to have done. Not bad on a mechanic's wages. He continues his tale.

"I got the tiger as I've been known to be a beast who likes ripping flesh apart. Thought you should know."

I have no time for the semantics of baldy's ego. I state my case.

"Gentleman, I think introductions are done. The motor's on a meter and I haven't got all day to hear tattoo tales."

I look at them both. The black guy nods to the heavy and he goes to the back of the garage. I can't see him. I check my surroundings. A nail gun's a short stretch away. I shift my feet and gain a few inches closer to it.

"Cup of tea, bruv?"

"Milk, two sugars, cheers."

"Lenny. Three teas whilst you're there. One with milk, two sugars."

"Yes boss."

"So, my man. I ain't seen you before. The big man usually sends a different runner for this type of thing, you get me."

"Maybe his usual's taken a holiday. I just do as I'm told. Ask no questions and all that."

"Sweet, bruv. I'm cool with that ya know. He's a good man. Generous. Know what I'm saying."

I say nothing in reply. Time fillers aren't my style. Lenny returns carrying three mugs of tea. He's slopping the hot liquid over the sides. A packet of unopened digestives in his teeth. He's carrying nothing else. He puts them down on the bench and drops the biscuits from his mouth like a gun dog on a retrieve. He shakes his burnt hand; he moves towards the Evoque and drops under the engine block. He reaches up. I move towards the nail gun. He brings out a black, oil-stained muslin bag and comes back to where we are. I take a sip of tea and keep the mug close.

"Put the toy down there, Lenny." The boss man indicates the bench I'm leaning on.

"Go on bruv, take a look at the piece."

I look at Lenny and nod at the parcel.

"Open the bag."

Lenny looks at the smiler.

"It's good Lenny. Do what the man asks."

Lenny puts on surgical gloves. He brings out a 9mm Glock semi-automatic pistol. It's pristine. He looks it over smiling. His index finger is near the trigger guard as he turns the barrel towards me. I look at his eyes and they're focused on me and he isn't smiling. My tea grips to his face as I throw it and grab his right wrist turning his hand palm up and high over his head. I pull him towards me and as he bends over I kick him in the mouth. He drops to his knees. I have him pinned by his arm to the floor my foot between his shoulder blades. The Glock has fallen to the oil-stained concrete. I tread on it. I grab the nail gun and stick it at Lenny's temple.

"What kind of fucking shower are you? Move another muscle, Smiley Culture, and Lenny gets a head full of nails."

Lenny's head is on its side. His mouth crushed into the oil-stained floor. Blood trickles out of gaps in his teeth like he's just eaten a beetroot sandwich. He isn't trying to get up.

Smiley is backing up, hands in the air.

"Boss, get him off. I was trying to prove it was no replica. Boss, boss, tell him for fuck's sake."

In his muffled speech is the desperation I want to hear.

"Easy, easy, big man. Put down the nailer and have a biscuit bruv. It's all cool. He's right. He's a simple fella man but wiv' a heart of gold, bruv'. Now for fuck's sake lets have us some tea and wrap this shit up. I've no beef with you. Your boss paid good money and this is his, I want it gone, understand?"

I look in Smiley's eyes. His gaze is steady. No swallowing or attempt to avoid me. I let go of Lenny and his arm drops to his side. I grab the cloth and pick up the Glock.

"Thanks for the tea. I'll see myself out."

Smiley stands aside. I put the Glock in the bag along with a roll of gaffer tape and some spare surgical gloves.

"Wait. You'll need these." Smiley opens a Snap-on tool box and hands me five full magazine clips.

"Where's it going?"

Smiley looks confused.

"How the fuck do I know?"

I feel a prick for asking.

"Till the next time then." I take my opportunity and leave. I'm not concerned about the camera. They won't be reporting this to any authorities.

I feel nervous and alone. I'm in Highbury with a semi-automatic and five clips. I exit the same way I came in and take a back route to the car. Fewer people. Less trouble. No filth. I try and keep my pace steady. My breathing is laboured. I inhale deeply and regain control. I did what I had to. I had no choice. This job is bigger than me. Once I was in the garage I couldn't refuse to take the gun. As far as they're concerned I knew what I was collecting. To hesitate is a lifetime's rumination.

I get to the street where I left the car. It's deserted. I stop and lean on a wall. No one is behind me on foot or in a vehicle. I activate the key fob. I put the bag in the boot with the spare wheel. It's too risky to try and conceal the gun anywhere else here. I drive towards Crouch End. I feel hot and the air-con cools me. I have to remain alert. I start a running commentary in my head of what I'm observing. What I don't want to see and hear are blue lights and two tones.

A saviour for some, a slayer for others. I have no intention of being captured tonight. I can't account for the firearm until I've called in. I can't call in until I find a callbox. A mobile is not a suitable mode of communication for this call. Who knows who could be listening despite my best efforts to keep the phone clean? By clean I don't mean in a designer case and well-polished.

I reach the top of Hornsey Rise. Traffic is good, no police visible. Once I reach the Broadway I know there will be a callbox. I see one. I turn into Crescent Rise and kill the engine. I wait. The area is deserted. No one has followed me in. I feel secure in the callbox despite being exposed in the street. I make the call.

"Hello"

Different response. Same voice.

"It's Sky. I have an issue."

"Go on."

"That last job, the one you provided the motor for."

"Yes."

"It was a fucking piece. A 9mm Glock and five clips. It's now in the boot of my car with no owner. I need retrospective RIPA authority to purchase."

Typical. No reply at the other end. Only a steady hum of breathing.

"Oi. Did you or did you not fucking hear that?"

"I did. You need to get rid of it."

"No shit, Sherlock. Why do you think I'm calling in? Get someone to the drop box in an hour, it'll be there."

"You don't understand. You can't give it to us; the whole operation will be lost. Big H is expecting that gun. If you don't deliver, it'll look suspicious."

"So, let me get this right. You're telling me to hand over a Glock and ammo to one of Scotland Yard's most wanted? You must have known what it was. You left a grand for me."

"The money's yours. You've earned it. Now phone Stone and find out what she wants doing with it. If you get found with it, by any police officer, you're not to call. You're on your own. Do you understand?"

"Fuck me, this is rich. You recruited me for this job. Good for me you said. A step up the food chain. Do you realise how much I'm out on a limb here? I need shot of this shooter."

"Stick to the script and you'll be alright. We've spoken long enough. Deliver the gun and move on. You're in no position to back out now or turn on us. We're bigger than you, Batford, and don't forget it."

My superintendent is silent.

Line's dead. A drunk is outside banging on the door, rubbing his crotch and waving a can of lager. I wait for him to get closer and open the door into him. He stumbles back, flat on the floor. His can of lager raised above his face. Nothing spilt. I step over him and drop a twenty-pound note. I need some air. I need to think. The Broadway is scented with the sweet aroma of Indian food. I walk up Hornsey Lane towards Sunnyside service station. I stop at a bench and call Stoner.

She answers on the fourth ring.

6

"Hello, who is it?"

"Hands off cocks and into your socks."

"All right babes you sound a bit fucked off. You got insomnia or something? Or did you just want to hear my voice before you drop off?"

I resist the urge to throw some fucks in and remain focused on the job, as I'd been instructed.

"I've got the parcel. Where do you want it?"

I can hear the rustle of clothing in the background and what sounds like the creak of a bed. I think I can hear snoring. No other background noise or voices. When she gets on the phone she's whispering.

"Fuck me, that was quick. Did Ghost not tell you?"

"You know he didn't. He never knew where it was going. That would be fucking suicide for me and him. I wouldn't be calling you back with the news would I? I've done my part of the bargain. I want rid of this tonight or I get rid myself."

"All right keep your fluff on. I'll call Ron. Meet him at the lower car park Ally Pally in an hour. It won't be quicker, he's got to get his fat arse out of bed."

"You mean you're screwing him? Wake the fat bastard up!"

"Funny. Speak tomorrow. Ron will call me later."

She sounds stilted. I guess I overstepped the mark. I just need to get rid of the gun, get back to Elephant and Castle. A long day, I'm done in.

Back in the car, I turn out onto the Broadway and turn left into Park Road. I can see headlights behind me and notice the silhouettes of two males in the front. Every car that passes lights up the interior. I keep a steady speed of thirty miles per hour. The car gets closer. It's plain clothes police. Both cops are in their early twenties. I can tell from the ballistic vests pushing out the neck of their T-shirts. I get a brief view but I instinctively know. I also know they are shadowing me whilst they call in a uniform car to effect a stop. Why else would they be interested in a nondescript car with one male on board driving legally? My mind begins to race. Have either of the guys at the garage grassed me up? Ludicrous, as neither had seen my car and no one followed me to it.

I see a garage up ahead and wait to pass before looking in my rearview mirror and pulling over. If it's nothing they'll pass. Maybe glance across at me but just drive on. They don't. The car mirrors my movement.

They know they can't officially request me to stop. They aren't in uniform. If I stop they have the choice to engage or not. I wait, engine still running. The interior light goes on. Passenger door opens. Cop One steps out. Radio in hand. I still wait, hoping. Then it happens. Driver gets out. Five feet...four...three...two, both coming at each side of the car. Cop One now shining a torch in through the rear window. They're both at the rear of the car. I engage the auto gearbox's sport mode and floor it.

The car leaps to life and goose tails. I can see the officers in my rearview mirror running back to their vehicle. I feel guilty. I have no choice. I forget them and concentrate on the lights approaching Muswell Hill. They change. Green turns to amber, turns to red. I look right, nothing towards. I look left, single vehicle parked, ready to move. He's looking at me and remains stationary. I'm over the junction heading towards Alexandra Palace. I have to lose this car. Every second counts. Police will be everywhere soon, looking, searching. I have no backup. No get out of jail free card and an automatic pistol in my boot with five clips of ammo. I turn into the first car park. It contains a single car, windows steamed up. I park on the far side. I access the boot from inside and grab the bag. I put on some surgical gloves and release the fuel cap. In the bag is the cash. I stuff some of it in the fuel barrel and light it. It takes. I stay low and head towards the rear of the Alexandra Palace ice rink.

The car parked up is leaving in a hurry. The night air's getting polluted with flame and smoke. I'm just hoping it's enough to spread to the interior before it's discovered. Whatever happens the modern copper is too health and safety aware to get close to a burning vehicle and that will buy me time before the London fire brigade arrives. Hopefully it will have exploded by then.

The bag is slipping off my shoulder as I scramble up the grass embankment and reach the top services road to the Alexandra Palace building. The view of London is amazing from here but I have no desire to sightsee. I stick to the building line and out into the ice rink car park. The parking is light; a group of kids are sat about drinking and smoking weed. They pay me no attention. As I cross the car park I spot a black cab in the lower section. I recognise the plate. It's the one Ron drives.

I don't rush towards him but use the cover of the surrounding trees and hedges to get closer. I use the rear of a VW Camper Van as a temporary rest point and to observe the cab. The camper's interior is fogged up with condensation and the suspension is going through a service. The occupants' minds won't be on the outside environment. Ron is the only occupant in his cab. He's picking his nose and reading the racing pages. I make my move.

Ron shits himself as I rap on the window. He drops his paper and releases the rear door. "Fuck me, why didn't you phone and let me know you were here?" I ignore the stupidity of the comment and get in.

He turns towards me. "I've gone to the liberty of providing a jacket and hat. They're on the seat. Stick the toy with me up front."

I willingly hand it over and change jackets. The one he's provided is a smart grey cotton, casual not business. The hat is flat peaked and matches. I look like a hip photographer on his way back from a shoot, minus his camera.

"Where to?" Ron's eyes meet mine in the rearview mirror.

"Holiday Inn, Finchley."

"Right you are."

As he moves out into the top car park we approach the junction and he turns left towards Wood Green. He knows not to go towards Muswell Hill. Blue lights fill the cab as we turn. Three police vehicles scream past. One is a dog unit. I was lucky. Ron reaches into a glove box and brings out what looks like a handheld CB radio. He flicks it on.

Control from Yankee One, on scene. Car is well alight. Need fire service. Dog is deployed and tracking, no sign of suspect, over.

"These scanners are great. Twenty notes from Tandy." Ron flicks it off and we continue towards Muswell Hill via the back roads and towards the North Circular. We don't say much. I just stare out the window and Ron drives. He glances back every now and then but the male intuition acknowledges nothing needs to be said. He gets to the hotel entrance and stops. I'd already taken what was left of the cash out of the bag. I hand him the BMW keys.

"Get rid of these as well will you?" He nods. Before he opens the door he turns around, his big bulk just skimming the wheel. "The big man likes what you did at the garages. He says Ghost had it coming. Zara will call you."

I get out and we shake hands. He leaves. I get my phone and punch in a number. It rings out and she answers on the sixth ring.

"Who is this? Do you know what time it is?" The voice is that of a sleep-deprived DCI.

"Batford. It's oh two thirty hours. Meet me at oh nine hundred hours, Lloyd's Cafe, Finchley Road. Breakfast's on me. I've got something for you." I hear rustling as she finds some paper. A pen moving back and forth in an attempt to draw ink. A disgruntled male's voice in the background. She must work harder on this marriage.

"I've written it down. This better be good." She hangs up first. Privilege of rank.

I enter the hotel lobby and see a public telephone. I dial. This number rings twice.

"Yes."

"It's taken care of. I meet with the DCI tomorrow. What do you want me to tell her?"

"Tell her the job's coming off in a week. Tell her the firm will be tooled up. Tell her you know no more."

"A week? What the fuck are you talking about, a week?"

"The parcel's on the move. You're going to be asked to drive a lorry. You'll do as you're told. DCI Winter will be kept suitably employed."

The line goes dead. My mind is spinning. I have no idea what's happening or who I'm working for anymore. All I know is that I have no way out. I have to see this through to its conclusion. I feel like the prey and no longer the hunter.

Called this morning at 0230 hours by DS Batford.

He was abrupt and gave the following message:

'It's Batford. It's 2:30am. Meet me at 9, Lloyds Cafe Finchley Road. Breakfast's on me. I've got something for you."

I terminated the call as he sounded rushed and not in a position to speak.

I recorded this entry at 0233 hours unable to date stamp log due to being away from office.

I will meet the officer as suggested and see what he has to report.

The rest of my team will continue to cover the cab used to transport our target.

Entry concluded.

7

Torrents of rain assault Lloyd's Cafe's glass. Each drop drums out its own rhythm on contact. I'd taken a cab to the venue, not Ron's. The last thing I need is to be wet and cold today. I have no idea what today will bring. The cafe is complete with the usual clientele. The kind of clientele I'm happy with but ma'am will have to adapt. As I stare out nursing a mug of tea waiting for her to rock up, I have the lyrics to James' 'Sometimes' going through my head – *The rain floods gutters, and makes a great sound on concrete.*

My thoughts are interrupted by the bell above the door as it's opened and DCI Winter enters. She's dressed in tight dark blue denim jeans and fitted black T-shirt, black Barbour biker-style coat. She's done well. No one turns. If they do they get a good look at her arse then carry on eating. She sees me and sits opposite. She ruffles her hands through her wet blonde hair then ties it back with a band from her wrist.

"Have you ordered?" She grabs the menu.

"No, that would be rude of me."

"Okay…I'll have the full house with extra bacon, I'm starved."

I follow her lead and order. The waiter brings over our teas and takes away my empty.

"So, is this where you bring all the girls then?" She's looking at me over the rim of her mug.

"Only the ones I don't want to be seen with."

She's still smiling. She has a sense of humour.

"Husband forgiven you yet for the rude awakening?"

"He has. Not that it's any of your business. Are you married?"

"No. Never have been, never will, so don't think of proposing if yours goes belly up."

She ignores my last comment. I would've too.

"So, what have you got to tell me then?"

She won't be smiling for long.

"Let's set some ground rules. If someone comes in here who knows me, by another name, you just sit and say nothing. I'll do the talking and get rid of them. If someone comes in who knows you, then you tell them you're having a meeting and will call them. You must call them back. Tell them you were speaking to a builder about a new patio."

"If someone comes in here knowing me, it will be a miracle. I'm from South London. The North gives me shivers."

"We must be prepared."

Our breakfasts arrive. She gets the ketchup first. I go for HP instead.

I start eating.

"So, what can you tell me? You've only had the action a day."

She seems mocking in her tone.

I wipe my mouth on a paper serviette, looking around before replying.

"The load's on the move. You've got a week, maybe less, before delivery. The firm have a gun. I'm no further on the female in the photo."

She stops eating and leans in. "A week? A gun? That's not right. Who's told you this?"

I look at her. She knows the question was absurd. There would be no reply.

"Look, that's not what's coming over the lines. We're hearing talk of multiple weapons, not one gun. How do you know it's only one?"

"I have it on good authority."

"Well, that's no good to me. This is the last thing I need. Why should I go with you over what's being discussed by phones?"

"What else is being discussed?"

She eats before responding. The fact she's admitted they're tapping a phone is something she should never have done. She has no option now. She's given me the rope to hang her if I desire. I don't though.

She's a quick eater. Comes with the job. You never know when you're going to get called away. The work waits for no food. Over the years I've developed a fireproof mouth.

"Okay, I haven't got any choice. I'd made my mind up after the way I behaved yesterday to let you in. I phoned your commander. It was the wrong thing to do. She told me if I wanted to stay in my job, I'd better cooperate. This operation means everything to me; to make the bust. You have to understand my superiors are looking at me to make this happen. I want the next rank and intend to get it on merit and good results."

"I could have saved you a load of grief if you'd just called me and asked to meet. My commander hasn't even met me. She knows this job though and that's why she's listened to those who told her to put me on it. Don't go sticking your head above the trench line again. She's a great shot."

The cafe has emptied nicely. A few regulars are left downing tea and toast, engrossed in copies of The Sun. I order two more teas and formalise my ethos. Once the teas arrive, I begin.

"I have to know everything you hear. You don't know and can't know what I'm doing or whom I'm speaking with. The integrity of this operation depends on it. Bottom line, we both want the same end game. That's the seizure and the firm put out of action. My remit is far from yours. It doesn't take a detective chief inspector to work out that there are other interests in your operation. Interests of national security."

I say nothing more.

She continues. "You're wrong in your assumptions of me. I'm a detective, yes, I may not have all the experience you have, but I've been hunting this man since he first crossed my path on the Regional Drug Squad. I thought once I was on the NCA with all at my disposal I'd nail him. That was until you showed up and pissed on my parade. We have different remits but I hope the same goal. Work with me, that's all I ask."

She's almost pleading. Self-deprecation momentarily surfaces on her face then leaves. I have to show some level of cooperation and empathy towards her goal. After all we're on the same team.

"That's what I am doing and will continue to do. I called this meet didn't I?"

"Your update will help. I'll have to bring an armed surveillance team with me now but that won't be an issue. What are you doing after this?"

"What are you offering?"

She relaxes and a brief crease appears at her mouth.

"You think you're a charmer don't you? You think that because I've been married more than once and focused on my job that I'm an easy target for you? You haven't got the class or manners to be of interest to me."

I sit back and laugh. Fair play to her, she's right, I haven't the will or the inclination for married cops. I've seen the pattern on numerous occasions. The playful banter at an office drink, hours spent together on a case, late nights eating out together, then bam! Life blurs into a fantasy that Disney couldn't even add sparkle to. Average fling, three months tops.

"Thank you for your brutal honesty. I was merely thinking about another cup of tea, maybe some cake."

"Just thought I'd be clear. I know how you like to be succinct and to the point, Sam."

"Don't your kids get sick of you never being there?"

Harsh, I know but had to be said.

"If I had any I'm sure they would. Tropical fish are my

husband's thing and that's enough responsibility for me. You? Many child maintenance payments to service?"

She's leaning back, arms folded.

"Touché. None actually. I'm a rare breed in this organisation, single and no responsibility or history following me. I'd have thought your homework through my files would have told you that?"

I've dampened her ardour. She appears reflective, a suitable response considering her remarks and any possible effects. For me, I feel nothing. A part of cop banter, nothing more. She is a sad indictment of human dedication to an impossible cause. A wish to rid the streets of crime using a morale-drained team with no money and limited resources. I prefer the teams I'm on.

She's conceding. She looks at her watch.

"I've got to run. Thanks for breakfast and keep in touch."

I can't resist the final word.

"Fish need feeding?"

She grabs her bag and jacket and with a flick of her hair, leaves. I have no intention of going just yet. It's going to be another long day. I grab the bill, pay, then head back to Elephant and Castle and await my call.

Meeting went ahead as arranged with UCO – DS Batford.

Meeting took place at Lloyd's Cafe 0900 hours.

Meal taken not claimed on expenses as DS Batford paid.

He stated the commodity was on the move and I had less than a week. The group are armed and he has not identified the female in the photo supplied by DS Hudson.

He alluded to know more but I made an error of judgement by:

a) Telling him I'd phoned his commander.

b) Stating I had line room support for the operation and that it didn't corroborate what he was telling me.

He claims he is working with me but I do not have full trust in this. In light of his information I will now apply for an armed surveillance team, as I have no choice if the shipment is moving.

This will delay my current tactics and mean I must pull my team away from all targets.

I am unclear whether Batford means one of the team already have a gun or there is only one gun being brought over. He doesn't fill me with confidence.

Current surveillance hasn't produced anything other than a budget deficit.

Something isn't right when the phones are telling me one thing and he is telling me another.

His source must be on the periphery of the crime or he's being asked to perform a role I am not being made privilege to due to national fucking security.

I'm also tired having awoken in the early hours, had little sleep and the world's worst breakfast. This may cloud my judgement at this time.

Entry complete.

8

"Alpha One, this is Six Zero, come in, over?" I can't hear a thing above my breathing. The earpiece is shit, the mic maybe broken. The estate's tower blocks rise above me like a beacon of oppression. I stay crouched behind a large concrete pillar. I can smell propellant hanging in the air's whispers. A colleague to my right is doing the same thing, his 9mm Browning is out and held down by his side. His breath is short from our last sprint to safety. We haven't been seen. Our objective is almost over. In the distance I can hear sirens. Sounds of glass against concrete and every now and then a larger crash as a heavier object connects with the earth. Shouting emanates in the distance. I pull the bandana up around the lower half of my face and look around the pillar.

There it is. The briefest glint of reflected light from a tenth floor window. He's there. His lair has been found. I wait until Alpha Two looks in my direction. He does. I indicate five showing my open hand and point at the block. It's twenty metres away. I count down using my fingers. I wait for his signal. He raises his fist then lowers it. He runs first and enters the main doorway to the block. I follow. Staying close to the ground and using the cover of burnt out cars as I cross the war-torn street. Flames dance off bonnets and the remains of petrol lick the road alight and engulf stray car tyres.

The immediate street's empty. There's a reason for that –

no one wants to die. I hear the sound of smashing glass and a scream coming from a first floor flat. We press on up towards the tenth floor taking the stairs. We have our firearms drawn but keep the face covers on. We blend in with the surroundings. Covert urban mercenaries. We're at the tenth. I open the main doors to the balcony and look left and right. It's deserted. The view is desolate. Fridges that have been dropped from the block lie shattered below. Cars overturned and ablaze. No fire unit is attending. They can't, it's unsafe.

Alpha Two is behind me now. I identify our target premises. From my jacket I take out two flash bangs. We have one chance. One job. Seek and destroy. I feel light headed; I remain alert awaiting a signal. My earpiece comes alive.

"Alpha One, from Control. We have you by satellite. Your location is good. You're cleared to go, I repeat clear to go."

The first flash bang goes in through the broken glass of the window. Alpha Two kicks in the door as I throw the second. I hear a double-tap shot. I'm in the room through the window. Target is on the floor in the hall. A rifle lies on the living room floor. I meet Alpha Two in the hallway.

"Alpha One, from control heat imaging shows premises clear. You have a moving target coming from balcony, be advised."

I turn towards the open frame to the flat's door. There he is, a boy of nine. He's looking at me. His eyes a thousand-yard stare. He raises his hands and I see the gun. I freeze. He shoots. Alpha Two falls. I raise my weapon as I crouch for cover and depress the trigger. The boy takes the force of each 9mm bullet as it tears through his small frame. His body twists as he gets thrown into the balcony wall with every shot. Blood excretes from his mangled body and starts filling a drainage gully. I put Alpha Two over my shoulders and reach the stairs, taking each step towards the roof at an even pace. I feel nothing. My body is numb.

The helicopter hovers overhead, I run towards it and Alpha Two is taken from me as I'm dragged in and we rise into the air. I hear the pilot through my earpiece.

"Control, we have both units on board. Alpha Two is KIA, Alpha Two in state of shock. Medi Vac, over."

"Medi Vac received. You are cleared to return to base with both units. Brigade commander is aware. Control out.

I can't breathe, I'm suffocating, I hear the whump, whump of the rotors, they grow louder, louder, LOUDER.

I sit up from my bed. I'm sweating. The overhead ceiling fan is on. I'm alone in my room. The only other sound is chanting coming from the main prayer room. I collapse back and wipe the tears from my eyes.

Maybe I'm tired. Overworked, struggling with the degree of responsibility. I've always taken responsibility for my actions. The boy's death is a constant haunt I can't shake. His face returns the more stressed I find myself. The dream has become the puppet that dangles at will whenever I feel the pressure. Pressure to finish whatever I've started. How much should one have to take to serve and do the right thing? I should have reacted quicker and killed the boy first. That's what happens when boys play a man's game. You're in the frame for death and death is the unseen enemy.

The morning's breakfast weighs heavy in my stomach, as does DCI Winter phoning my commander. Last thing I need is her breathing down my neck as well as Winter. Sitting up, the weight shifts. I sit at the edge of the bed and hold my head as my neck aches from stress and feels heavier than it should. The gas valve has been located and the heat is turning up.

9

A workout is what I need. To feel alive you have to move your body. Chest and arms the order of the day. Early afternoon feels cool but welcoming. The free weight area is empty apart from the usual gym bunnies and steroid swallowers. I go to the locker to change and on opening it there's another padded envelope. I grab my shower stuff and put the envelope in my bag and put it back and go shower.

They know I'm here. That's what's disconcerting. The budget cuts didn't affect my firm. Money is no object as long as they get results. A mockery when across the country officers are losing wages, jobs and posts. A five-year plan of destruction. Government controls the wrecking ball. In the end you have to pick your side. Morals won't pay bills. It's not that I don't have any, mine are different.

King's Cross. Gateway for the prosperous to leave. Pavements paved with silver for the prostitutes. My car has been left outside the coroner's court. A fitting place to leave it. They've left me a VW Golf GTI. I swear they're just enjoying attracting attention to me. It's early evening and I have a post-workout hunger. As I approach the car a local Tom is propped up against the wall by her right foot blowing smoke rings. Sad to realise if she had a choice that's all she'd rather blow. She looks at me and winks. I nod back. A reciprocal acknowledgement rather than an agreement for work.

She looks relaxed for a woman about to be screwed all

night by a mix of married men and tourists. She doesn't look my way but casually remarks, "I'd rather be paid to look after those stiffs than the stiffs I have to face every fucking night."

I smile in response and start to open the car door. She's not interested in where I'm going or why I'm there. She recognises pain and angst. She has a doctorate in it. She doesn't need to know any more.

I'd like to help her. I can't. We both have to continue surviving on the street. She has her way. I have mine. We think we have time to do what we want before we die. It's a lie. If that were the case why would people with cancer have 'visit Ikea' on their bucket list? I get in the car and examine the envelope. There's another £1,000 to replace the wad I torched along with a scanner. I can't afford to get caught with a police radio. The near miss rattled me. It's good to know what your pursuer is saying and who's coming to back them up.

I put the scanner under my seat, put £500 in the glove box and roll up another £500 and put an elastic band around it. I whistle to the Tom and drop the roll on the floor as I drive off. She sees this and takes no notice of the car. I look in the rearview mirror, her hand is over her mouth, she's sitting on the pavement, her head obscured by her black shoulder-length hair. Her shoulders slumped, moving up and down.

It appears like a good kind-hearted deed. In effect I ensured she wouldn't mention me or my car if ever asked. I also can't afford to be stopped and have to account for £1,000. Proceeds of Crime Act is all an officer needs to remember to take it off me and haul me in. I don't need that kind of attention. The heat is already on simmer. If I were in Grand Theft Auto, the cops' heat level would be blinking and I'd need to change vehicle. I have done that and it still feels unsafe.

I head towards Camden but looking to sit up in Cafe Rouge in Highgate. Instead I reach The Flask pub and sit outside. The atmosphere is convivial for someone waiting for a call. I finish my second Scotch when the phone goes on the table. It's Stoner's number on display.

"Alright babes. You free this evening?"

"Depends. What's up?" I don't wish to appear keen.

"Thought you might want a drink after the other night?"

"What would your man have to say about that, I wonder?"

"I'm a free woman. Well, tonight anyways. It's not social. I can't speak on this though. Where are you?"

"Meet me At The Flask, Highgate Hill, in thirty minutes. Tonight may be difficult."

"Cool. Vodka and Coke for me. I haven't eaten so don't make it a double."

She's gone. I scratch the continued growth of hair on my head and face. Seems strange to have it back after so long. I don't miss shaving. I stay where I am. I'm comfortable and the evening's warm with the outdoor heater next to me. As I watch the world go by I wonder how I ended up going from walking the streets of a war zone to the streets of London as a PC. I'm so far removed from those days I barely recognise myself anymore. My aspirations have disappeared, any hopes I may have had long forgotten. Each day has become a challenge of survival. A new urban warfare where there is no apparent regulation.

Thirty minutes have gone and she appears. Ron drops her off then goes. He nods at me and waves. She smiles as she sees me. Her eyes look fresher than the previous meeting and the dark glasses are gone. She bends over and kisses me on the cheek. I don't reciprocate but don't dislike the engagement. Her lips are soft against my stubble with a brief but purposeful linger before departing. She drapes her coat over a seat next to her and puts her clutch bag on the table. She makes a point of showing me the battery from her phone before putting it back in her bag.

"So, lover. How have you been since you threw your teddy in the corner?"

"Good. I've slept and that's a bonus."

"I hope she was good." She reaches out for a cigarette I'm offering and accepts a light. Her lips are accentuated by a deep plum lipstick. Not every woman's taste but she knows she can carry it off.

"How long have we got this time?"

"Is that what she said?"

"Very good. Until your driver turns up?"

"We've got plenty of time. Lots to fill you in on, like I said on the phone. Things are happening quicker than expected. It's all good but Big H needs you. He's not begging or nothin' but he don't take no for an answer when you've already been given a job. He says it's disrespectful."

"Go on."

She relaxes and takes a drag of her cigarette and a slug of her drink. She doesn't hold back and goes for another. I order the same again and wait. This part I find the strangest. The joining together in a guilty act. An act that has more consequences, financially and of liberty, than a quick shag and who gets the house and kids. This kind of partnership can end in death. Death isn't high on my hierarchy of needs. She returns with the drink and crisps. Salt and vinegar. Class.

She throws me a packet and we open one right down the middle and share. The romance is not lost on me.

She's in the seat next to me now. Her toned thigh is against mine. I don't move and neither does she. It's good for appearance, if nothing else.

"Let me tell ya what's goin' down and it ain't my skirt."

The story she relates makes sense. Big H is getting pressure from way up the food chain. The guy at the very top is sat on ingredients for a cake he doesn't want to bake. He's happy with the recipe but now wants shot. There isn't anyone that will move on this deal without having a slice of part of the product. Big H is one of these. He wants a taste before he commits. He's like a king who has a chief taster. The taster for Big H is called Sugarman. Sugarman just needs the parcel to conduct what's known in the trade as an MOT. If the parcel makes the grade and passes the checks the main haul can then start moving. Where do I come in? I have to collect and deliver the parcel to Sugarman. All sounds straightforward – except that Sugarman is in Pentonville prison.

"How in the fuck do you expect me to get charlie into the Ville?"

She looks at me. Her face says it all. "How the fuck do I know? I deliver the message, you sort out the problem. The amount ain't big, a baggie full. Enough for Sugarman and his little shop."

She looks around sits back and takes in some early evening sun. She carries on talking as she takes in the vitamin D. Her shades are back on and obscure her eyes, which is a shame as they're beautiful when she's not coming off the sniff.

"If it's good he'll call me and I'll tell Big H. After that it's all on. Job's big and that means good money. I wouldn't mess you about with anything shitty. I don't know no more right now as he keeps his cards close to his chest. But he only moves in bulk and large amounts of it. He's been talking of retirement after this one so it must be fucking huge."

"What's in it for me? I've done one job and seen nothing. So far it's promises and wind."

I wasn't expecting the next move. Stoner reaches into her handbag by her feet. I can feel an object the size of a hand brush on top of my leg. It isn't a hand, it's an envelope so fat that it's incapable of sealing.

"Expenses rendered and all that. He don't normally do part payments but appreciated the way you handled the last job and wants to keep you on board."

I move the wad and store it under my upper leg against the seat. I have a jacket I can put it in but nothing else and the pressure against my leg is enough to tell me this is about £2,000 in cash. He must really need me. The gun was worth £1,000 tops even with clips.

"Tell him thanks. How long have I got?"

"You've got twenty-four hours. Sugarman is expecting the package. He works the gardens. He loves his horticulture. Sniffing flowers and gathering the pollen. The last bloke lobbed it over the wall and got caught. So that's not an option. I'll leave it with you but he expects to find it outside. It's up to you how you get it in there. Are you gonna get me dinner then or is crisps the lot?"

"I'll shout you some nuts. You don't look like a dry roasted kind of bird, salted suit you? I've gotta work." I drop her a £50 note, kiss her on the cheek and go. The prison is across town and although I've passed it and been in it, this is different and time is running out. I need eyes on to plan my next move.

10

I'd left the car in Highgate. Tube, bus and my own two feet will be my transport from here. Traffic's calm and as the bus makes its way down Caledonian Road I stare out of the top deck. My mind's churning over the solution. I have one in mind but it will take planning and every minute counts at the moment. We stop outside the tube entrance and a black guy, twenties, black hoodie and Nike Air basketball boots climbs up and sits behind me. He's listening to drum 'n' bass on what appear to be a new pair of Beats headphones. Behind him is a whiteguy, well built, same age but making his way along the bus aisle with a purpose. I can see him in the window's reflection. His eyes are everywhere. He's conscious of where the bus will stop next. He's not sitting. If he was looking to jump off at the next stop he'd wait downstairs.

The guy behind me is oblivious to his surroundings, music his only solace at this time. The standing man moves his hand towards his pocket as the bus slows for the lights. He pulls a knife and holds it to the man's throat behind me. "Give me the phone and the Beats, now."

I move across to a seat opposite. "Now! You fucking shit! I SAID GIVE EM UP!" The man seated is frozen, his brow a creased page. He doesn't know what to do. In fairness, I do but don't need the grief. I just hope he gives them up. Fat chance.

"Yo, bruv." The standing guy looks at me then towards the front of the bus as it moves off. "Just let him off, move onto someone else."

"Who the fuck are you to tell me who to rob, you spic fuck."

Spic, that's a new one.

"No need to get personal, just saying that's all." I turn away. He's still looking. I make a point of checking the time. I can see in the window he's clocked the fake Breitling. Not even he could tell it's fake from the distance between us. He lets the man go and moves towards me. Never bring a knife to a fight if you're not prepared to use it properly. He broke the first rule by approaching me from the side, knife arm out. The brakes of the bus provide good forward motion, for me not him. He staggers forward. I grab his knife hand and smash it down on the seat rail as I get up. This brings his head closer to the solid metal edge of the bus seat. His forehead connects with the edge on several occasions. I carry on smashing it against the chrome until the knife drops and claret starts spraying from his split nose. I cannot afford to get blood spattering on my clothing. He passes out in a heap on the floor.

I nod at his first victim who gets up and follows me down the stairs as we alight at the next stop. I point out to the driver through the open window that there's a man upstairs needing medical aid. He turns off the ignition and puts on his hazard lights.

The man behind me has waited and walks with me a short distance. "Cheers, man. I…I…didn't know what was happening."

Why would he? Not everyone in London has been mugged. I simply nod and leave him. I go into a newsagent's. He doesn't follow me in. I make my way towards the prison. My public deed done for the day. No one on the bus will give a statement. Why would they? Justice has been served. One man's crime is another man's passion.

The intervention has delayed my progress and I'm a stickler for time when it's on my watch. Good criminals keep good time. The higher up the food chain the more business-like the venture runs. Most of the top men I've met will not answer a call after five p.m. They have a life outside the office. A wife, children, mistress to attend to. Me? I work when required. I'm required more than I'd like to work. If all goes well then my career won't be a long one. Take your bus mugger, he had it all wrong. You don't pick a heist on a London bus, it's full of people, the bus has cameras and there will always be some have a go hero who will have a go. The game is high risk. Ideally he should have ditched the knife in favour of an item of clothing like a scarf, wrapped it around the guy's neck, choked him till he blacked out then taken his Beats and phone. Not in public, of course. A simple follow off the bus would have presented an opportunity.

I don't study this kind of behaviour. Why waste an education on what is obvious and common sense? I don't need a degree in criminal psychology and cognitive science to work out the bus isn't a viable option for a quick gain. Am I bothered about the CCTV? Have you ever seen an image off one of their cameras that identifies the assailant? Also why would the old bill chase the hero when they have the mugger and the knife? That is unless he dies of course. By the time I reach the prison the light is fading. The steady hum of engines is constant as commuters escape the city. The prison gates are closed defying entrance and exit. There will be no vans ferrying the detained today.

The outer wall is three times my height and I have no intention of scaling it. I'm all for getting the job done, but not at any cost. I've seen what I need to see and must find an internet cafe that's open. I head back towards Seven Sisters and Holloway Road. I'm guaranteed finding one there. It doesn't take long. The cafe is full with one spare booth. I pay my money and log in. Across from me is a middle-aged guy who's obviously looking at porn. His left hand is in his pocket and he's not playing with change. I put this out of my mind and bring up a Google satellite map of the prison.

Zooming in I can see an area that Sugarman can access,

and will have an excuse to. It looks like it's full of bags of building sand. I check my email. Nothing. I find the Argos site, order what I need and leave. I have time to collect today.

The plan is this: I now have my £400 drone that I intend to fly over the wall, lower into the sand area, where Sugarman will collect the baggie attached to said drone. The drone will come back to me courtesy of the return home function. Clever? I hope so. The kit has a camera so I will be able to see and record it getting collected via my iPhone. Hopefully the bum I paid twenty pounds to collect it for me won't be pulled in by the old bill should they trace where it was bought. Now I need the cocaine and the luck of the gods.

I have about twenty minutes flying time to get airborne, over the prison to the drop point and back without anyone noticing. The drone has a range of two kilometres and will auto take off and land, if I need this. I phone Stoner.

"Aye, aye lover what's up?"

"I need an appointment for the MOT, tomorrow at ten a.m."

"Okay. I'll let the mechanic know."

"Tell him I'll leave the motor near the building sand area. Tell him to look up at the clouds at ten a.m. and wave if it's clear."

"Fine. You about after? I'm free for a couple hours whilst he's taking it for a test."

I don't want to but I have to. The quicker Sugarman feeds back the result then the quicker I can move this job on or not.

"Sounds good. I have a hospital visit later. Meet me in the canteen at Great Ormond Street Hospital. At ten thirty."

"Okay, babes, laters."

"I need the motor to take to the testing station..."

"Shit. Yeah, no problem. I'll get Ron to bring it over in an hour. Where will you be?"

"I'll wait outside Tufnell Park station, he can pick me up

there."

"Alright, see ya tomorrow."

The line's off.

I can't help noticing the longer I speak with people like Stoner the more my language develops into abbreviated street bollocks. I need to keep up to date with it so I can't complain.

I need to clear my head and walk towards Tufnell Park. Ron is on time. His cab approaches from the East. He doesn't see me but I watch as he's looking around. He pulls over outside a kebab house. As I look, no other cars pull in or pass that could contain surveillance. The junction couldn't be covered by one person. Too many points of exit that would need covering by cops on foot and in cars. I step out from the doorway I was propped up in and flag him down as he starts pulling out again. He pulls over, I jump in and he kills the 'for hire' light.

He looks fucked. Bags under his saggy-skinned eyes. He never seems to change clothes. Bedecked in a Lacoste polo shirt that looks as if it was second hand when he got it. His nails are bitten down and the nicotine-stained fingers are engrained more than a Charmouth fossil. I settle back and he drives off.

"Where to?"

"Vauxhall station."

"What? Fuckin' Vauxhall! I hope you've got the cash."

"Drop the bill on Zara, I need to get there."

Ron is gazing at me from the rearview, shaking his head like a drugged pit bull. If he owned a dog it would be a British bulldog. Like owner, like dog. The fat fuck would never walk it. It would sloth wherever he lived and eat fish and chips and god knows what other takeouts the slob lived off. I don't like Ron. I'm finding it difficult to trust him. He's done nothing to make me doubt his credibility, but let's just call it gut instinct.

We reach Vauxhall Bridge and he's said nothing more. He's looking at the Argos bag but hasn't asked what's in it.

We arrive at Vauxhall and I get him to drop me outside Tesco. I need milk. I get out and he leans over and hands me a small padded envelope. He nods and drives off. I look around me and all appears as it should. No obvious signs of being followed. No unwanted attention. I flag down the next cab and direct them to home. Milk can wait. I need to store the envelope. Who's going to run the risk of raiding a Buddhist community to look for drugs? Not the law, anyway.

It feels good to be back in the sanctuary of the centre. The people's lives here flow like the positive energy the monks imbue. For me it doesn't rub off. I'm happy with my set of laws and abide by them. They're simple, really. Be of service. Do what it takes to survive. If that means harming others, so be it.

Brief, I know, but they've served me well so far. Society has created too many laws. It's no wonder people end up breaking them. Law enforcement is changing. The five-year cuts are kicking in. I'm only doing what the public really wants but is too afraid to say. On the outside it may appear to be a selfish pursuit, but really I'm only doing what anyone else would, given the opportunity. If those guns and drugs were to end up in the wrong hands chaos could ensue.

I put on another pair of surgical gloves and assemble the drone. The controller is on charge. I managed to get some duct tape from the centre's handyman. I secure the parcel of cocaine to the underside of the drone with the tape. Secure enough that Sugarman can remove it without instructions. I have no time for a dummy run.

Tomorrow will be a busy day. Cometh the hour, cometh the coke. Lewis "Chesty" Puller, would not approve. I decide to eat with the community this evening. I need to switch off; my mind is mayhem and its after five p.m. so the clock's stopped. Eating here is an interesting affair. The cafe has a fresh selection of vegetarian and vegan fare. A welcome break from the shit I've been eating. I select the quiche and salad and sit at a four-place table. I eat alone. I don't feel I give off a vibe of 'don't come near me' but I'm clearly not on the reservation list. I eat and become aware of someone joining me. I stop mid-mouthful and look up to see the resident monk sat opposite. He's not eating. He won't eat again until tomorrow morning.

He says nothing and neither do I. I adhere to etiquette when I'm a guest and joined by the resident owner. He breaks the silence.

"It's okay to speak. This isn't a silent retreat. How are you finding your accommodation?"

"Wonderful thanks. A lovely room with no view."

He laughs heartily.

"Yes…yes. A cell with a view would be most unkind to a person." He drifts off, looks towards a statue of the Buddha and sips some water.

"I'm afraid your stay must come to an end, my friend. You have a week to find other accommodation. We have other students who need the bed and you seem reluctant to join us in study. I hope you understand."

He gets up and leaves the eating area, his maroon robes embrace him in a gentle hug and for the first time I feel I've met someone who intuitively knows humanity and its flaws. I'm aware I'm one of the flaws but can accept this from him. Even a Buddhist monk has his limits of tolerance.

I finish my meal and take it over to the kitchen. On the way I collect others' empties and find myself at the sink filling it with warm water and washing up soap. I remain here until I've washed all of them. Another young person dries and another puts away. We say nothing. Each of us lost in our own worlds. I would invite no one to visit mine. I shake that shit off and grab a coffee and head to bed. The phones I'm carrying are my heaviest burden now.

11

I'm awoken by the melancholy voices of twenty or so retreat-goers chanting at different tonal levels. Not so much a call to prayer, more a snooze button in its final stages of death. My head is clear. I slept well. The ceiling fan is off and this seems to have alleviated the dreams. I sit up and check my watch. It's 0500 hours. Time for work. The advantage of living here, other than it's free, is the endless supply of coffee and tea that well-minded decent people ensure is on tap. I dress appropriately before going to get my first cup. By appropriately I mean I cover up what shouldn't be shown to strangers. Not in this setting.

They're all in the main gompa gaining enlightenment and I grab some of their prepared fruit breakfast and take it back to the cell. I refer to it as that, as that's what it is. If this cell could talk it would talk some shit. Some comedian had left a copy of *Crime and Punishment*. I had started reading it and continue whilst I wake up. As a child I found comfort in words. They would drown out the sound of my mother screaming as my father let loose with his fists. Sven Hassell was a favourite. Apart from where her screams coincided with screaming in the book. That shit was too real for me.

I check my phones. No calls from Stoner or work. DCI Winter hasn't contacted. I need to rectify that. The air outside is fresh and a factory worker nods as he makes his way home from a nightshift. I can tell a shift worker by their look. Tired and hungry for sleep. The street is as I'd left it.

No change in cars, nothing new overnight. My home is safe for the time being. I find a call box.

I dial 0800 555 111. A male answers.

"Good morning, Crimestoppers how can I help?"

"A guy called Guardino is looking to bring in a huge amount of drugs and guns. It's due soon. He uses a driver called Ron. Ron drives a black cab. Tell the NCA."

"Do you have a reference number for this sir or is this the first time of calling?"

"Just pass it on, okay?"

He repeats back what I've said.

"Thanks for the call, sir. Have a nice day."

I intend to have an awesome day, once I've had a proper breakfast. Not around here but at an Italian cafe near King's Cross. All the cabbies use it. They bitch more than a short-changed hooker. You can't beat the banter though. That call should get DCI Winter running around. The beauty of Crimestoppers is that no one can trace it back to you. NO ONE. Not even my lot. I cannot find out who made the call, from where or on what number. Winter may not know this, but she will soon find out. I don't want money from them. They're a charity and I see this as a donation.

The drone and drugs are secure in my osprey brown leather man bag. Osprey being apt, as the commissioner has decided to source a firm that uses eagles to take down drones. I love wildlife but not an eagle in an urban setting hell-bent on disrupting my day. Another example of police cuts. A winged wonder taking over the fight against crime. I have a suit on that I only wear for court appearances but serves its purpose being in the vicinity of the prison. I could be taken for a brief or a cop. Neither of which I mind. The cafe is quiet. The regulars are all away using their timeshares in Tenerife or out fleecing tourists. I grab a cab and head towards the prison. It's 0830 hours. I can't be too early and can't be late. The cab drops me at the gates at 0915 hours – the traffic was slow no matter which route he took.

The wind is light, which suits my purpose. The sky is

mottled with clouds but no rain is forecast. Another bonus as I have no plan B. I walk away from the prison and find a park. It's deserted and well within my two-kilometre flying range. As long as it stays this way for the next hour I should be fine. I grab a coffee at a nearby cafe close to Caledonian Road station and wait for my time to come.

It's now 0950 hours and I'm back in the park. A local is running his dog. He has a phone to his ear and a fag in his mouth. Every now and then he animatedly points the cigarette at the sky whilst shouting obscenities into the phone. Not a good sign at this time of day. After two minutes he's had enough and growls at his dog, who follows him out of the park and away.

I sit at a bench and get out the drone and the iPhone. Each one is primed, ready to go. The app loads in my location and a press of the screen sets the come home function. Both are on and the drone's camera shows a picture of my nose hair on the iPhone's screen as I check the package. I launch the drone and watch the screen. I control it as the camera shows me the roofs of the houses and the street adjacent to the prison entrance. It's gained good height and you'd have to be looking far up to notice it. Its 0956 hours. I manoeuvre it over the site where I'm hoping Sugarman will be. A black guy is talking to a screw near the landing site. The drone hovers but I'm conscious of time. The black guy is well-built and has neat corn rowed hair. He shakes the screw's hand and the screw walks off. The black guy then looks about and walks into the sand area picks up a shovel, looks around again then looks up and waves.

That's my signal. Not subtle but, hey, needs must. I start the descent. He sees what's happening and the drone's camera captures a beaming smile. That smile immediately fades as the same screw enters the yard. I work the control panel and get the drone up again and away. My heart is beating fast. I have limited time and if Sugarman is put off, the job could be too. I have to make this work but it's out of my hands and in Sugarman's to get rid of the screw. I move the drone back over to see what's happening.

The camera's zoom is incredible and as I switch the zoom up Sugarman hands the screw a series of notes. The screw then leaves and from my vantage point, disappears. Sugarman resumes shovelling sand and looks up again and nods. The nod means yes, go ahead. The drone now drops and proudly I land it in Sugarman's shovel. The camera goes fuzzy and I see distorted scenes as he frantically gets the package off. He then tips the drone's camera and plants a great wet kiss on the lens. I press the return home button and start packing away. My work is done. It's 1005 hours as the drone returns to the park. I have no further need for it. I rip out the camera and the computer chip that controls it. The rest I throw in a large commercial waste bin.

I grab another cab and make my way to Great Ormond Street Hospital. En route my work phone goes. DCI Winter's number appears on screen. I answer.

"Hello, ma'am. How are we this morning?"

"Where are you? Something's come in?"

"Oh, I'm fine thanks for asking. I've business to attend to."

"I need you back at Spring Gardens. Office meeting at two p.m."

"I'll see what I can do."

"You'll be here, Batford. Two p.m. sharp."

"Look, I'm in the middle of something right now. If I can get back for that time I will. Alternatively, you can buy me dinner and bring me up to date."

"Ask your mother to get your dinner. Be at Spring, two p.m."

"I can't ask her. She's dead."

I kill the line. That part is true. Let her stew on it, or if she's really caring, she'll call me back. Twenty minutes goes by. As I expected she's a heartless bitch. The journey was good and as I get out at the hospital's entrance I feel elated at this morning's excursion. It had better test positive and the purity good. I need this job to come off. Deals like this take time and planning with a high-risk element. Never ever let it be said crime doesn't pay. In the foyer, a photographer is snapping a C-list celebrity holding an oversized cheque. Another product of a fabricated entertainment industry, prostituting itself to the greedy masses of uneducated fuckwits who buy into it. Still, if it benefits sick children, then who am I to complain?

I go past the meeters and greeters and carry on past the reception desk turning right towards the main eating area. As I walk along the corridor various children pass me. Some in chairs with tubes in their noses, some on foot but clearly struggling. Families desperately seeking solutions accompany each one. This is one place where empathy resonates within me. It's also here where I see strength and resilience beyond what my imagination can conjure up. A place where anyone could challenge you to see who had the most on and only a fool would take the bet.

I know this place; a colleague had a child treated here. I would come and visit his kid when he couldn't and drop him off and wait for him when he could. I use the word colleague loosely; he was a snout of mine who did a good job. It didn't last long. He's dead and his kid's in care. Even pond life has a heart. The restaurant is quiet, as the lunchtime rush hasn't begun. I pick a table at the back of the room and get seated where I can see who's coming in. Stoner arrives on time. She sees where I am and comes over. A steady rhythm emanates from the floor as her heels connect with it. She's dressed like she's going out for lunch. An expensive handmade dress reveals her sleek shoulders. Her hair is resting over her right shoulder revealing her neckline. She's smiling. A good sign.

She sits down, leans over and kisses me on the forehead in a way a concerned relative would. Fitting.

"I had word from the garage. It's passed, you'll be pleased to hear."

I nod and smile. "So, lunch with your lover then?" I ask.

"I thought we only had time for coffee?" A smart riposte. "He's taking me to some posh hotel. Says he's got business to discuss on the back of this morning. He's told me to tell you to be available. He likes your work and says you're on the firm. I'll know after today what's happening. It all looks good though."

"Great. I can't wait to hear what he has for me and how much he intends to pay. What are you getting out of all this then, besides his cock every night?"

She smiles and frowns. "It's all about sex with you ain't it? You think that because I'm blonde with decent tits I'm no good for anything else? I do well out of him. He pays me a decent wage and don't forget who's meeting you each time. Yeah, I have to take a slap every now and then but that's just him. I'm his arranger. I arrange what he needs and I produce what he wants, when he wants it. He'll pay you well and he never defaults. How do you think he's stayed in the game so long?"

"He can't pay you that well if you still live on an estate in North London."

"Where I live is no concern of yours. I tell you what you need to know. Let's leave it at that. Where you off to then? A funeral? Who's here you know?"

I lean forward and she mirrors me. "Where I'm going is no concern of yours and who I see here isn't either. Let's leave it at that." She's looking me straight in the eyes. Her lips are close enough to touch but we both resist. She breaths out and her breath dances over my face. It's sweet, not foul.

"Touchy bastard."

She gets up and I sit back. "I'll call you this evening and let you know what's what." She blows me a kiss, winks and leaves. She's purposefully working the floor as she exits the eating area. She knows I'll be looking.

Nothing heard from DS Batford. I haven't contacted him as I have nothing to update him on and it's him who needs to get used to calling me with the intelligence he's tasked to get.

Armed surveillance requested and authority being granted and team availability has been made available to myself.

No other talk over the phones. All seems to be on.

Crimestoppers have passed a log from an unknown caller who asked for the below information to be passed to the NCA. I have asked for clarity as to where this has come from but I have my suspicions. I believe this is from DS Batford as the caller asked for it to be passed to the agency. I cannot prove this at this time. We have assets talking to police about our operation and it MAY have been given by one of them although this is very doubtful, as the information is specific:

A guy called Guardino is looking to bring in a huge amount of drugs and guns. It's due soon. He uses a driver called Ron. Ron drives a black cab. Tell the NCA.

Above passed to intelligence desk for research. We are already aware of this information from other intelligence feeds.

I will contact Batford later this morning and request he attend the 1400 hours briefing arranged for today.

Entry ends

12

I stay around GOSH and sit for a while in a park in the middle of a square of houses. Pigeons irritate the diners, begging for scraps. Anxious parents stare at their phones and hope. I don't use a smart phone, as a rule. Why anyone would want a device that can tell others where they are or what their favourite pastimes consist of is beyond me. Same goes for social media. Sure, I use Facebook, Instagram, Twitter but only to research the people's lives I need to infiltrate. The iPhone for the drone was for just that job.

When did I go from being loyal, true and trusted to a self-serving cleanser of filth and scum? An outsider may see me as out for myself but I see myself as doing some public good whilst getting paid. That's from both sides of the fence. The fence is wobbling though and I need to secure it. I have no family to turn to. I've tried relationships but when you leave in the middle of a date not explaining where you're going or just lying, your chances of recidivism are thin.

By the time I've left Holborn and arrived at Vauxhall I'm in no mood for meetings. The tube was mobbed and I feel as though I've just left a frotteurs annual convention. Coming up for air feels good. How Orwellian of me. I ignore the leaflet being thrust towards me like a fencer's foil as the escalator reaches the top of the station. I do succumb to a samosa and a Mars Bar from the small confectionary. A man's got to eat.

By the time I surface, my ears are greeted by the sound of

sirens and the city grabs my senses with its usual pollutant grace. I avoid Spring Gardens and make my way to Tintagel House, a tall building next to MI6. This place used to be home to many of the Met's finest teams. It's now in disrepair and abandoned, much like myself. The security guy looks up as I exit the revolving door and nods as I press the lift button for the third floor. The floor is unoccupied. It was previously a Child Murder Major Incident Team's offices but they'd long since been kicked out to smaller and less convenient accommodation. I carry on walking down the corridor looking at discarded desks and old phones.

"We're in here." It's a distinctive male, Scottish voice. Not one that grates on you but one that has depth to it and could never get on your tits. I enter the room. The two people I was expecting are sitting on upturned packing crates looking out over the Thames as a frogger boat exits using the ramp. Incredible amphibious craft, if you're a tourist. The Scottish voice is Mike my detective superintendent and the other person in the room is my commander. She pushes an office chair to me with her foot. I dump my bag and coat and take off my tie.

"How are you?" She's polite but the small talk is only an icebreaker. She doesn't have long. You get to that rank and your whole life is split into identifiable periods of time. The length of time varies with who you have to see and who you don't want to see but have to. I fall into the latter bracket. She authorises my deployment and all I do in it. Well, she should, but it would appear from my last contact she has changed her mind on that aspect. I respond with good grace.

"Alive. Could be worse, I could be deployed undercover for the good of the country with absolutely no backup from my employer… Oh that is the case… Isn't it, ma'am?"

Go for the throat early in these exchanges. With a woman like the commander she doesn't appreciate bullshit.

"Cut the shit, Batford. You've cost me a car and caused me a lot of grief with the commissioner. It's fun not telling her what the job is but she's getting sick of the cost both in manpower and money."

"Manpower? It's just myself and a desk jockey. Do either of you appreciate how big this fucking job is and what I'm being asked to do? Or would you rather not know until we get a result and get paid out?" They both look at each other like climbing buddies claiming the other was bringing the rope. She's pissed off though as she's up and looking out over the river her hands on her hips. Good hips, mind. Never had kids and never will. The job is her baby and she intends to have it suckling from her till she dies.

"This isn't an everyday job, Batford. That's why you're on it. We need someone we can trust to get the job done with the minimum of fuss and backup. I will continue to support your legal deployment. Anything above and beyond that and you're on your own. We made that quite clear in the beginning. The surveillance commissioner is getting twitchy around the purchase of guns, that's why I knocked back the last one. You also realise we can't be seen to know everything. That wouldn't be lucrative to us in the end. You did a good job though. It got to the right person. For the record I would rather you didn't refer to your detective superintendent as a desk jockey. We all have a role in this and as much to lose if the job doesn't come off. We all have mouths to feed, Batford. Tell me the next stage. I don't need to know how you've got there unless you think I do."

I light up a cigarette. Neither challenges me and both just look in my direction and wait. I skip the prison drug supply. They won't want to know about that.

"The main job is on. I find out later what my role will be and when it should all come together. Zara Stone is my person close to Guardino and she seems to be his runner. Bali worked a treat, no one suspects anything. They have a driver called Ron who ferries them about in a black cab. I've never met Guardino and it sounds like I won't. I don't trust this Ron. He makes me uneasy. They have a guy called Sugarman in the Ville. He's their chemist. If the stuff's good Guardino will roll with it."

I take another drag on my cigarette. Neither of them makes any notes. I break the brief silence.

"I've got a meeting in an hour at Spring with DCI Winter. She's becoming a problem. She was all over me in the beginning and now she's backed off until a call earlier. I've an idea what the meeting's about." Neither looks my way but the commander pipes up.

"The one I got a call from? Winter, Klara Winter? Very good at her job. Ruthless, in fact. She's been hunting Guardino for a while now. She will stop at nothing until she catches him. I will warn you she will be finding out, about now, that her intrusive surveillance authority won't be renewed by the secretary of state. We've acquired that facility now and will be listening to Guardino. Good job you won't be talking to him. Your Miss Stone will be though. Loose lips sink ships, Batford. Don't let it be yours. Let Mike here know when you know more. He has some cash for you and a change of car. Let him know where the last one is and I hope it's roadworthy. I've dealt with your last pursuit with the law and the burnt-out vehicle. Nothing will come of it. Tell Winter nothing. Let her rant over the loss of the wiretap and she will lean on you."

She nods at Mike and they both go to leave. I write the street name down where the car is. He hands me an envelope and I put it in my bag. They leave and I wait. They know I can't back out. They have my head on the block. One carries the hood, the other the axe.

As I enter the tunnel of the railway arch towards Spring Gardens I wonder how this next meeting will develop. I long for the day I attend one and I feel glad I turned up. Actually, that's a lie. I'd rather not go to any. No detective enjoys meetings unless it's about more overtime or more staff. Sadly, those days are gone.

The entrance to the building was easier on this occasion. Same security guard, different drill. Amazing what a laminated piece of plastic can do for access. It works cutting cocaine and slipping a Yale lock and can get you into a secure area. No, I haven't faked an ID; I've actually been issued this one. I place my phones in the same locker outside the room and knock on the door. I don't have access to the office. I can't blame her; I'd do the same. DS Hudson opens the door and beckons me in. There's no music. The time is 1415 hours and she's already begun.

"Good of you to join us, Batford." There's a hint of sarcasm in her voice. I scan the room. The team has increased in staff. She's had the message about her knockback on the phone authority and upped her staffing levels. She's on a mission to nail this guy and I need to focus on my game.

"Thanks, all, for getting here. I hope by now you've taken the opportunity of bringing each other up to speed. The intrusive authority has been knocked back. I have no option but to adopt a conventional route and that means loads of money for you lot, as the hours will be long. I expect the budget to be managed properly and I expect regular and current intelligence feeds."

She looks at me when she says this. I look at my watch.

"It would appear we have a friendly who's contacted Crimestoppers. Guardino is planning to move soon. He also has a driver called Ron who ferries him around. I have a meeting after this with Crimestoppers where I will ask them to divulge their source. Any update on who this Ron is?"

I smile as she states her next meeting. A geeky researcher waves from the back. All thick-rimmed dark glasses, tank top and no hair.

"He's Ronald Stewart. He's got previous for GBH, armed robbery and kidnapping. He's never been stopped in that cab. It's not licensed for hire. It would appear he only uses it when he's picking up Guardino or any associates. Further analysis of the cab shows a pattern of two cars that have shadowed the cab on five different occasions in the last month. One of these vehicles is a black Range Rover Evoque, the other a black Porsche Cayan. Both cars are leased to different individuals. We're working on the names of them now. No pattern or preferred route. My suggestion is that Guardino has a team around him for protection."

Now that was worth coming to the meeting for. Being out all the time it's easy to miss bits of the jigsaw. This was tiny but key for me. I need to know my adversaries both on the inside and outside.

"Thanks, Craig. I want two teams out today. Locate this cab and stay on it until further notice. Keep me and the command room updated on all movements. That's all."

"Batford, a word in my office."

Being civil because of the new company, no doubt. I get up and follow her. Her desk has changed. It's full of paperwork. She's drowning and I've no intention of throwing her a ring.

"What do you have for me?"

I'm tempted to say flowers but the look on her face suggests she'd have hay fever. I'm cautious since my previous meeting with my commander, but she expects something and she's entitled to it.

"It's early days but I've heard Guardino is looking to move quicker than expected. He's had a sample tested and he's happy with it. As soon as I know more I'll let you know. I'm on this job full time until it's finished. I do need to know when your team's out though. I can't get caught on the plot at this early stage."

I've gambled with that. If she doubts me she will refuse. If she respects me she won't. "Like you said, different remits. You're on your own. Call me with any updates any time of day or night. That's all, Sam."

Using my first name to soften the message. Fuck her. I will do this my own way. In the words of the late Brian Clough, 'I may not be the best manager but I'm in the top one'. May the best team win.

UCO, DS Batford, attends meeting late, arrives 1415 hours. I'm noting times due to his lack of diligence to my requests and for any further disciplinary procedures should I see fit.

I included information in the briefing to assess his face. I also need to cover my back should he be into any of the targets mentioned. I have to be mindful of his safety after all.

I also fed in the Crimestoppers information and he smirked. This only goes to affirm to me it was him, although he and I know I can never prove that, despite me saying I would pursue it.

Let him think he's up against a novice. Hardens my resolve and will hopefully make him less surveillance conscious.

I've increased staffing and surveillance capacity. I have taken the decision in light of guns being mentioned and the SCO35 ambivalence to keep me in the loop. I have no option but to consider DS Batford as part of my line of enquiry. I am aware it goes against the grain but I've been left with no options as it would appear events are unfolding quicker than expected and DS Batford is closer than I gave him credit.

13

"Mum, where's my jumper? I'm freezing."

"In your bottom drawer where it always is."

"But I can't find it. Can you help me?"

"All right. I'm coming. I can't keep doing these stairs all evening running around after you. Your dad will be back soon and I need to get his dinner on… Here it is. On the floor next to you."

"I tricked you! I wanted to show you my drawing I did. It's when we went to the beach, just you and me. Look, there's a boat and someone fishing. Do you remember that day?"

"Yes. Of course I remember it, it was one of the best days of my life. Oh. That's the door, your dad's home. Right, you need to tidy this room up and I'll go down and see what he wants for his dinner."

"Okay, Mum. Love you."

"I love you too."

"Gillian! Where are you? I'm starving."

"I'm upstairs. I'm coming down now."

"Why are you up there and not bringing me my dinner? I said I'd be home at eight. I'm coming up."

"No, please don't. I'm on my way. Dinner won't take long. I've put a six pack in the fridge for you."

"Who made this mess? Where is he?"

"He's in the toilet. He's just clearing up. He's been drawing, that's all. It won't take long."

"Oi! Come out of there now and tidy this shit up. I've told you before what would happen if your room was messy. I'm going to count to three and if you're not here I'm coming to get you. One...two...thr... Wise move. You've had all the chances I'm prepared to give. You're not listening and I fucking hate people who don't listen, especially little shits like you. You're only here because the social pays well for us to have you but you've disrespected this room and it's time for another lesson in manners."

"Dennis! Dennis! No, not the belt again. If you mark him we'll get nicked. Just calm down and have another beer? I'll get it for you and make up for not having your dinner ready later. What about that?"

"Take your shirt off lad and put your hands against the wall, back facing me. The quicker you do it the quicker it will be over."

"Jesus, Dennis, leave the boy alone he can't take another beating... Please...please leave him for all our sakes he's just a boy, he doesn't understand! No, Dennis! NO...MY GOD PLEASE STOP YOU'RE KILLING HIM!"

"Sir? Sir? Are you okay?"

"What? Holy shit where am I?"

"You're in the library. You have fallen asleep but were shouting out as if in pain. I hope you don't mind me waking you, but I couldn't bear your suffering any longer."

I sit up and wipe the saliva from my mouth. My head is hazy, confused, I know where I am, I know the monk in front of me, but I cannot focus. I need to prepare for work. I check the time, it's 1900 hours. I relax, I have time. He waits whilst my breathing returns to normal. He's sat opposite just looking out of the window. What the fuck he's looking at I have no idea. He has fallen in with my breathing pattern, or I have fallen in with his. I begin to feel lighter as the nightmare leaves. I move my back in the chair. I still feel the ridges where my skin was broken. The scars have faded physically but still haunt me mentally. I now feel like a patient in a therapy room whose chosen to catch up on some

Z's rather than talk.

I get up, bow and leave. I never thought I'd do that with any sincerity. I go back to my room. The water from the shower wakes me up and I feel back in the game. The hunter has returned and my prey beckons. Tonight will be different. Winter has her team out and Stoner is unaware. Winter is like the snow, beautiful in appearance but cold and harsh the longer she hangs around. I have no intention of her blowing me out but every intention of showing her team up. It's my job. It's what I'm paid to do.

I check the phones. They're charged and primed. Winter hasn't phoned, I take that to mean her team is still out. I put a call in to Stoner. Set the evening's wheels in motion.

It rings twice and she answers in her dulcet tones. She sounds out of it. There's a nasal quality to her voice and a series of sniffs and coughs.

"Alright babes, what's up?"

"You sound like shit. I take it it's snowing with you?"

"Pure white, babes. I'm fucked. If you're after a meet-up I can't do it, but there's some work if you want it but it's tonight. I was gonna call you but I fell asleep."

Typical coke-head. She may look all serene but wave a bag of white and she's like Pavlov's dog. I'm disappointed. I need her on form or the job slows down and that's no good when the commodity has been set in motion. I've nothing else on though and at least I know Winter will be having a dull night.

"What is it?"

"This fella, we call him Charlie Brown on account of what he's into, he's got a lorry needs moving to an industrial site in Hemel Hempstead. It's cool; it's not loaded up. Ron can pick you up after if you want?"

"What's in it for me?"

"You're on the firm now, lover. The job needs doing and you've been selected. I told you before you'll be looked after. It's all part of the bigger picture. Look will you do it or not? I'm fading and need an answer."

Pushy when she wants to be.

"Ok, I'll do it. Don't bother with Ron, I'll make my own way back. What's Charlie Brown's number?"

She gives me the number and hangs up. I have a good memory for numbers and punch it in to the phone and dial. Its answered by a gravelly-sounding male voice.

"Charlie?"

"Yeah."

"I hear a lorry needs moving tonight? Been told to call you."

"Yeah. Get yourself down to Wembley Industrial and look for Guardian Skips. I'll meet you there. What's your name?"

"I'll see you there in an hour."

I never give my name over the lines. He should know better and I take it as a test.

14

Wembley Park station is the closet tube to my destination. I exit and wait outside. Watching, observing, ensuring I'm alone. Foot traffic is heavy, which is good for my movement but not for spotting cops. I look at the points that provide cover, a bus stop, cafe window, there's nothing obvious to me that would indicate a static surveillance. I set off on foot towards the industrial site.

As I enter, the large map board shows Guardian Skips as Unit 7A. There is no one about. All units have shut down for the day. A large industrial bin rattles as a stray cat emerges carrying a part-eaten burger. I can see a large metal slide door that's about twenty-feet high. Set to the side is a standard metal door. Cameras everywhere. I knock and wait. I can hear footsteps on metal and by the rhythm there's a staircase inside. Judging by the time it takes the feet to stop, it's large. The door opens and I meet my contact.

"Sky, is it? CB they call me. C'mon in." I ignore his knowledge of my name and enter the building. Even a fuckwit like him can make a call and use it to sound clever.

I step over the threshold into a vast hangar space that houses a fleet of skip lorries. None are new, they all look like they've seen service. Some are in a state of repair. The garage floor is immaculate. The kind of clean I've only ever seen in traffic police garages. Not what I was expecting for a firm that disposes of rubbish. We climb a set of metal stairs and I look up to see an office at the top suspended on a metal platform overlooking the work bay below. It's a good thing I have no difficulty with heights.

Charlie Brown motions to a seat as we enter and takes out a bottle of whiskey and two glasses from under his desk. I decline by telling him I'm driving and that brings out a wry smile over his round face. He's in his late fifties, six foot tall and built like a lorry. His bald head is shaved and he has a goatee. He's a hands-on manager, I can tell by the old oil on his fingers. He doesn't smoke.

We're both sitting comfortably and I wait for him to tell me what he needs to. He's sipping his drink and seems to be doing the same thing. He weakens first.

"Don't say much do you? What are you, a fucking mute?"

"I'm a man of few words. So people tell me."

"That's why he's hired you for this then." He's smiling. "You ever driven a Mercedes AROCS 1824 – BlueTEC 6?"

"I've driven many lorries. One blends into the next. I'll get the hang of it."

"You haven't, have you? I can tell a lorry driver from ten paces and you ain't one. Tell me why I should let you drive this one out?"

Good point, but he's overstepping the mark. I've been hired for the job and he must facilitate the request regardless of his preconceived notion as to my driving experience of heavy goods vehicles. I get up and move towards the expanse of glass that hovers over the works below. I lean on the window, my back to him. I'm safe; I'll hear him before he can get to me. It's these situations that separate the men from the boys. I'm no bully but I'm no pushover. I'm tired, hungry and in no mood for debate.

"Let's put it another way shall we?"

I turn towards where he's sitting drinking, leaning back in his boss chair looking like he owns the place. "The last person who attempted to educate me as to my ability ended up on the floor with a nail gun at his head and a mouth full of snot and blood. Now, I'm not threatening, I'm just explaining in as few words as possible that I need the keys to whatever vehicle needs moving and the address where it's to go. Let's just move on from the getting to know each other stage and onto the parting of ways."

Charlie Brown isn't happy. He's not used to being given direction. Like a sat nav being questioned by a driver. Pointless. I stay standing as his bulk rises from his seat. He cranes his neck forward and back and stretches his arms out wide expanding his fifty-inch chest. I remain still, assessing my options. Option A, move if he rushes me and let the window take him. Problem with that will be the mess and explaining the body. Option B, use my experience of boxing in the army and police and deck him. Option B it is.

This comes to nought when he finishes his Pilates routine, opens a desk drawer and takes out a vehicle key. He throws it at me and I catch it.

"It's down there. Take it to the engineering shed at Hemel Industrial. Ask for Pikey Paul. He'll take it off you, then phone Zara. For the record I respect your employer and know he's keen to get this moved. Your lucky day, you trumped up piece of filth. Darken my door again and I'll put you through it."

I nod in acknowledgement and descend the iron steps to the floor. Charlie Brown stays where he is, presses a button and the large metal doors flow to the side. The night air greets my body and I find the lorry. It's minus the skip. I climb the steps up to the driver's cab and put on some gloves; it's dirty work.

I was glad he didn't have a pop. I would never have stood a chance. I exit and turn left, heading towards the M1 and my next meeting with the unknown.

The chains on the lorry rattle as I hit junction 1 and head north. It's 2300 hours, the train to Bedford races me and takes over. I check the central dash. The gauge on the left shows that my fuel and speed are good. The right shows that the temperature is fine. Old habits die hard. A life in the Army and Police create odd habitual patterns and checking vehicles is one of them.

The cab stinks of sweat and graft. The pot below the stereo unit is full of biros for signing off invoices and hire agreements. The air fresheners hanging from the phone charger lead have had their day. I flick on the rear observation screen and leave it. It's down by my left and gives a great view of the rear of the lorry. The absence of a skip gives great observation of the road behind me and any interested cars I should know about. Right now all is clear as I settle in to the drive. I pass junction 6 and wait for 8 to appear.

As I sweep up the exit lane and approach the roundabout that leads to the site, I wonder what Big H intends to do with this lorry. I'm glad I don't know. If I'm asked I can genuinely respond and hopefully no further questions will ensue. I see the sign for the engineering works. Progress has been made since the Buncefield fire and the site is coming back to its former glory. I approach the front of the building, stop and turn off the engine and lights. As I'm sat the rear screen becomes distorted with car headlights. They stop behind me and go out. One person in the car. He gets out and walks towards my side. I'm higher than him and my door is locked.

He's smoking and the smoke swirls around him like a cloak as he nears. I wind the window enough to hear. He looks up and stubs the cigarette out on the footplate.

"You'll be looking for me?"

The thick Irish accent is a good start as is his skinny gaunt look and furtive eyes.

"I don't know. Who are you looking for?"

"Well now, there's a thing. A fella called Charlie Brown says he's sent his blanket over in a lorry for me. I think that'll be you. Now back it up and follow me."

I wind my window up as he scuttles back to his car. He leads me back to a mobile home and caravan storage park. It's not a gypsy site, it's used by anyone who needs caravan storing. The metal gates open and I follow him in. We move down to the far corner farthest away from the road and park up. I get out and lock it up. He's still in his car. He eventually gets out and comes over. "The keys?" I hand them over.

"I'll call Zara tell her it will be ready tomorrow night. Now, do you need a lift anywheres?"

"No, thanks."

"Suit yourself there fella. I wouldn't want to be out this late with nowhere to go. Them days are long over."

I'm already walking off. I know where I'm going and the hotel is only a short walk away.

15

"Shut the fuckin' door, I can't hear myself think. Sit, darn son, take the weight off. Brandy?"

The club's noise is drowned out as the door to the gym is closed. I take a seat as requested. Lenny is a skinny guy, ex-boxing champion with the ears and face to show. He's now in his early sixties. You wouldn't mess with him though. He pours me a glass and I wait to hear what he has to say. Big H didn't want me hanging around doing nothing so he lined me up some other business before the main event. This is good for me, as I won't be caught up with DCI Winter and her mob whilst they chase a taxi all over London and learn about Ron's favourite cafes and his addiction to Costa Chai Lattes.

Lenny was no pro boxer on the main circuit. He was one of the best street fighters and underground boxers of his generation. His idea of fun would be the last man standing after a ten-man fight and still shouting for more. I was looking at some of his pictures adorning his meagre office wall. He was a powerhouse for a man his size and you could see he had a vacant stare that would be enough to make a man think twice before stepping out from the crowd against him.

I'd only experienced that once. When I first joined the police, boxing was still a mandatory requirement. You couldn't police London if you couldn't take a punch or know what it felt like to be in a fight with no backup. I was okay.

I'd done milling in the army and I could take a hit and dish it out. But I would never forget the fella they paired me up with who hadn't. He was around thirteen stone, fit but not a fighter. Never taken a punch in his life let alone fight. We got paired on weight and I could see the others in the same weight range breathe a sigh of relief when they hadn't been paired with me.

I had no choice. The instructors were putting on our gloves and head guards after our hour's tuition, I'd made my mind up he was going down and it would be quick. No way I was letting him get a lucky punch in that would rock me. As we entered the ring the instructors gave us a brief talk about remembering the lesson and to keep it clean. I chose to blank that out. The instructor stepped out and we were told to go to our corners. The instructor then shouted, "FIGHT." I was out of my corner before he had left the ropes. A right jab to the head followed by a left and a right to the stomach ensured he went to the mat. The bout was stopped and he agreed to go on. He had a resilience in him and he wasn't about to give up easily.

The shout came again and out he came, quicker this time. I watched his gloves up round his face. He didn't want another hammering about the head. He stepped forward and I landed the right on his chin. He staggered and I went in for the kill. The red mist came down and I let fly with fists as he fell. I continued when he was on the floor with feet and hands. The instructors were both in and grabbed me, lifting me off my feet, and as they turned me away I could see him on his back, arms out wide. He'd had enough.

Boxing stopped after that bout. I was hauled in front of the commander for recruit training and admonished. Thankfully he was ex-army and saw through it. That and the other guy didn't want me fired. I bought the fella drinks all night in the recruits' bar and we partied. He accepted my background and that I couldn't let him hit me. Army pride for an unbeaten record still remained. He went onto better things in the job. I'm where I am. Now, I'm here in a boxing club in East London waiting for Lenny the Lent to tell me his dilemma for me to resolve. Since his move to Christianity he no longer engages in illegal activity but sees using others to do his work as a necessary evil.

"You box son?"

"I did years ago, not anymore, I've slowed down but can still swing a punch when needed."

"Good to hear. I loved it back in the day. Happy memories. So Zara says you're the man I need to resolve my issue. I hope that's correct as you can answer to her and her boss if it ain't."

He sips his brandy and nods at the closed door.

"I've good lads out there. Some of 'em fucking brutal but getting down to training and staying clean so I don't want to use them or damage my club's reputation. Some little fucker is trying to do me damage though and they need sorting out."

He's on his feet now and stands in front of a photo of him with blood streaming down his face from cuts above his eyes and lips and a gap where a tooth once was. His right hand is raised above his head by an old fella in a camel hair coat and trilby.

"See that? That was my retirement fight. Alexandra Palace. Not the main place. On the grassland over the road. Just me and Joe Malone. Biggest meanest gypsy fighter ever to be on the circuit. The money was good and in safe hands on both sides so we all knew the winner would get their cut. It was a warm July evening. Birds were singing, life was good. I was fit as fuck at that time. Never beaten. I had my doubts on this one though, my opponent was big but I was quick and many a man had fallen to my fists. The idea was we'd wait until evening then go to the grassland. Punters had been in the boozers all day and come from all over the country for this one."

He pauses and takes another sip. His mind is in that field.

"It gets to witching hour and they start to drift down. A couple of coppers are sat down on a bench having a smoke.

We ignore them. Before they know it two hundred are on the land ready for the off. We knew it would be quick, these fights always are. I'll give the cops their due. They knew they could do nothing and knew there weren't enough of 'em. So they took a couple of fella's jackets put them on over their blue coats and had a bet and watched. It was over before the blue lights and sirens stopped. You'll never stop the public phoning in. I downed him with one combination. He'd got me good though. Battered me about the head and stomach. The crowd were screaming, it was great. He gets dragged off by a mob whilst the coppers drop the coats, stick their radio batteries back in and start moving us off. I'd been moved into the crowd and was taken away for treatment by a private doctor. That was it for me. I'd beaten him. Made good money and wanted no more. That was ninety-one and I've never looked back."

He looks happy as a pig in shit until his mind drifts back to why I'm sitting here.

"I need you to sort out an issue I have. It's to do with me mother. She lives in a lovely block in Hackney. Has done for as long as I've been on this earth. The place has changed though and so have the residents. A group of Vietnamese have started a grow house in the flat below hers. I don't need to tell you the vermin that come and go and the problems it's causing her health. The heat troubles her breathing, see, and she's asthmatic. If I do anything she'll cop it, as they'll take it out on her. I need it shutting down and fast. She's over at mine but she's ninety-two and as much as I love her she's getting right on my tits. Here's the address. Make it permanent. Zara says her boss will sort it out with you. I like him, he's got a social conscience."

I take the address. I have a respect for the elderly and I've time to kill.

"Leave it with me. I can't promise no one else will move in after but I'll do my best."

"Good. That's all I can ask. The caretaker doesn't give a shit and I've heard he's on the take from the Vietnamese to turn a blind eye. I've nothing against them coming over here and making decent food but not this kind. They're bang out of order and have it coming to them."

He finishes his drink and pours another. It's only 1100 hours.

I get up and he nods. He isn't going to show me out. I walk back through the gym. The smell of sweat and breath the prominent scents. Leather punch bags being pounded and skipping ropes fizzing through the stale air. No one looks at me. All engrossed in their own worlds with no concern about anyone else. I turn up the collar on my coat and leave. I stand in the doorway first and observe where I am. Both ends of the trading estate, where the club is situated, are clear of foot and vehicle traffic. I cannot be too careful now. Winter has turned up the gas and has no reliance on cold weather handouts.

I'm conscious of time. I grab a bus and head east towards Southview Estate and Birkbeck Block where Lennie's mother resides. I get to the estate outline and alight. The vision is one I've come to know from many estates all over London. Poverty and social exclusion feed the need for revolution. The estate has become its own society over the years and from the various lookouts on verandas it appears that business is good.

Bins are overflowing where the rubbish chute can't cope. A rat disappears from sight as it burrows into the top of Mount Shitmore. The stench of fetid waste matter is overpowering. Nappies litter the ground providing solace for flies. The eyes from above are tracking me loosely. I'm dressed in a tracksuit that's seen better days and the coat is well worn. I've decided this should get me in. I also know whoever is running the grow house will either be coming down off last night or starting up again if they're up. I don't have time to wait until the evening. I find the block where Mrs Lenny lives. You can see how this would have been lovely in its day. All the blocks are built in a square with a small garden area in the centre and parking for cars. The balconies surround the inner square that overlooks the gardens and parking areas. It reminds me of the inner court of a castle, but absent of fair maidens.

The main block door is a buzzer system but 'trades' works. I hear the lock release on pressing the button and enter. The lift is out and I take the climb to the fifth floor slowly. Edging along the wall for a better view as I ascend. I've reached the fifth floor. I realise how high I have climbed and have no wish to look over the balcony below. Above me are another ten floors to the roof. Flat 52 is signposted with a cannabis leaf graffitied underneath. I'm guessing I've found the right one. No one is outside the door as I look down the run of concrete that leads me towards the entrance to 52.

The lookouts must be on a break or change over as they've disappeared. They were not for flat 52. I have no plan as to how this will go. After many years raiding them as uniform and on plain clothes drug squads, I've learnt to expect the unexpected. Systems have become more sophisticated for alerting the occupants to outsiders especially if the cannabis factory is established. Sentries, cameras and CCTV are becoming the norm. From across the quadrant loud heavy bass music thumps through the brickwork. Shouts echo around the block reverberating inside the concrete chamber. It's now or never. I approach the door.

The windows are covered over with plyboard giving the impression it's uninhabited. A sound of voices leaks through the door as I press my ear to the wood. It's a new doorframe and door. It's been raided before and had the door and frame smashed off. The sounds I can here are female and a male. Both sound slurred and are arguing, over what I don't know. I bang on the door. No response and the voices stop momentarily. I bang again.

"Fuck off."

Well I now know the male is still conscious. I bang again with my fist shaking the door in the frame and I hear the internal slide chain rattle. I hear feet approaching from the inside. One set only.

"Who the fuck is it?"

"Yo. Open up. The caretaker sent me."

"Well he can go fuck himself, I'm busy."

"He said something about new locks."

I wait. The voice is clearly thinking. His frazzled drug-addled brain trying to work out if he's asked for them or needs them.

Bolts are racked open and the door opens on the chain. A pair of bloodshot eyes peer round and a yellow-coloured gaunt face focuses as daylight hits the retinas.

"I don't see no tool bag and I ain't ever seen you before."

"It's too bait to send someone local. For fuck's sake let me in, I need to measure up then go get them."

The chain slides off and the door opens enough for me to gain entry. I slip on a pair of gloves. Precautionary. The smell is worse than outside. I'm not referring to the smell of weed; I'm referring to the smell of urine and faeces. I'm also certain it's not a pet. The walls in the small hallway are damp from humidity. The humidity, I'm surmising, is from the heat and water from the hydroponics system set up in one of the rooms to grow the cannabis. From the heat emanating throughout the hall I'm confident the harvest hasn't happened.

I move forward and skinny man puts a hand on my chest. He's topless and covered in black and grey faded tattoo work. No real thought as to design just whatever he could afford as he went along. His shaved head is sweating from the heat and there's a sheen across his upper body. I look at his hand that's on my chest, cigarette stained fingers contrast with the darkness of unwashed grime and soil. His fingernails barely register. He's cut for a man, I guess, in his mid-thirties. Cut from gear not from exercise. A twitch in his right eye tells me he's wired and not for baiting. The CZ-75 Star pistol pointed at my face also confirms this.

I'd faced this weapon before in the army at a similar range until a sniper rectified my situation. My face and body armour took the spray of brain matter but I felt the need to learn some more about the weapon and now I realise why. The thing about this pistol is its capability of holding one in the chamber whilst being capable of single and double-action firing. This one was live and not fake. It could also use a clean. Like I said, you learn to expect the unexpected – but I hadn't expected this.

"Hey. You don't need that, just let me do what I've got to do and I'll be gone."

His hand remains as his head throws back in a gurgled laugh. He spits phlegm on the wall and focuses back on me.

"You don't remember me do you Sky? I was a bit more with it when we last met, you know, I had a suit and hair and more teeth. Now we meet again and I'm the one in the driving seat."

My mind is trawling the memory cabinets shouting orders at the file workers to shift their arse and find me the memory I need before it becomes part of the wallpaper. Then it appears. The man I'm facing I last sat alongside en route to a buy bust of ten kilos of heroin, five years ago. I was driving. He was the courier of the goods. Tom Barnes, street name of Treacle. My memory wasn't happy with staying at that revelation.

"Turn left."

"This left?"

"This left. Keep going until you get to the coachworks yard at the end. They should be there in ten. I need to make sure we're alone"

"I haven't seen anyone following. All looks good to me."

"I pay you to drive so shut the fuck up and drive. When we get there you say nothing. Just stay with the car until I return. Same drill as before."

"Got it. The gate's open, should I drive in?"

"Yeah. Drive in and park up near the Jeep over there but swing this round so we're facing out. I want out of here fast once I've got the cash."

"Sure. No problem. I'll park it right here."

"This'll do. It all looks good to me. You're alright you, Sky. You

don't get flustered or nothin', just do the job you're asked to do. This all goes well, I'll throw another grand your way and you can keep the car."

"I've always dreamed of owning a clocked Volvo XC90."

"Cheeky bastard. Lights up ahead. Keep yours on until they come in and keep the engine running. Looking good… Yep… That's them. Right they're out. Pop the trunk and wait till I'm out."

"Sweet. See you in five."

This isn't looking good for me anymore. His eye's still twitching. A sense of urgency is crossing his pallid face. He's not in the mood for bullshit or bluffing.

"Fuck me, Treacle, I thought you was dead? 'Course I remember you, now. What the fuck happened five years ago? You walked off, I was desperate for a piss and as I got behind an old Transit the place lit up. The filth were shouting and screaming and running around all over the place. I ducked my nut and held out till the morning when they all fucked off."

His eyes tell me he's listening as he's looking into mine as I speak but he's not buying it.

"You think I'm going to take that, you dirty grass. You called 'em on to the plot didn't ya? Well now we're back again, you and me and I'm thinking who's coming through my door next. Strip and do it slowly."

Standard procedure for a gatekeeper of a grow house who suspects the locksmith to be wired for sound. Of course I'm reluctant to rent my clothing even though the heat is oppressive. I have no intention of leaving here naked but do need a plan and fast.

"You what? You think I grassed you up? What about all the other jobs we were on and nothing happened? Why me? I was there don't forget, waiting for you to come out! I'm hardly going to grass and have the old bill come to where I'm about to get a wad load of cash and a motor. You're off your head. Working here's fried your brain. Now we can talk all day long but I've got a job to do so put the piece down and let's get on with it."

"Who's that?"

A gravel-sounding female's voice emanates from a far room. She sounds drunk but odds on just stoned on a cocktail of drugs. I can hear the faint sounds of a child's murmur coming from the same place. The child sounds sick and definitely newborn by the cry.

"Shut the kid up and don't come out. I've got this." Treacle isn't happy either.

The gun has now moved up to my forehead and his face is in mine. The smell of sweet putrid breath spews forth as he speaks.

"Take your fucking clothes off now or I'm going to pull the trigger."

I have limited time to waste here. I acquiesce and strip, dropping my clothing one by one on the dirt-encrusted floor. As I move to remove shoes they stick to the linoleum hall surface and as I raise my foot a tile comes up with it. Treacle just points the gun and spits until I've undressed fully.

"Turn around slowly and bend over."

I do as he says.

"Happy now? Can I put my clothes back on?"

He's not replying. I'm reluctant to turn around fully. You are when someone has a gun trained at you. It doesn't matter how many times you've faced one, the feeling of imminent death is still the same. I turn my head only and keep my hands down by my side.

A glance at the smashed mirror on the wall and I can see him looking at me. He steps closer, the gun held loosely at his side. He then raises it and runs the muzzle down the scars on my back. I tense as it runs over the welt ridges that have grown with me over time. The curiosity has now got the better of him and he appears more relaxed.

"What happened to you? You look like you've been caught screwing an Arab's wife. When did you get the leg?"

"The welts are a life of beatings as a kid. The leg… I got shot. Now I'd love to chat but I need my clothes."

He appears happier. He lowers the weapon to his side and waves it at the clothes indicating I can put them on. No one outside the police has seen my leg. In my role, some disabilities are best left hidden. I've adapted with it and don't recognise it as a disability. I have a slight limp, nothing more. It has made me look upon life in a different way. A way that most human beings don't live by. I faced death and won by the fact the armed robber couldn't shoot straight. As he exited the jewellers, the shout was given to attack. All our gunships were on him as he came out. We knew he was going to be there. We'd known what he was planning for weeks and when it would be. Someone like me had befriended him and agreed to drive the getaway car. We weren't going to let an armed robber get back in a car with the undercover officer. That was never part of the plan.

It was all going to be easy. We'd stake out the jewellers, watch him go in and take him out in the act of the robbery. Right place wrong time for me. I was already out of the car, MP5 trained on the gunman as he exited the shop. I shouted, 'Armed police, drop your weapon!' He didn't listen and got a shot in. I got hit in the shin. He got hit twice by a double tap to the chest by my partner. He was dead before he hit the floor. I was in the air ambulance on my way to hospital. I got a commendation and a chat with the commissioner at my hospital bedside. He vowed to have a war on gun-related crime. The media never knew my identity. I just missed my job. They couldn't get rid of a disabled copper either. That would make bad press.

Treacle is the only person, on this side of my life, to know my secret. I was lucky in Bali as my stay was short and white linen trousers were the order of the day and I chose to wear shoes. The monks knew but didn't ask questions. I did what I've always done, adapt and overcome. This current situation is a bind though, as it can only end one way. I slowly put my clothes back on, the stench getting more pronounced as the lamps do their job. I'm conscious of a baby being here and I already know I can't leave the kid.

Treacle is now relaxed and turning towards the living room where the business end is taking place. He opens a door and a black plastic sheet bats him in the face as he goes in. I follow. The farm is well towards harvest, the leaves sway every now and then with the heat and he walks through the plants touching them with the gun and smelling them every now and then. At the far end of the room is a mattress on the floor and used works litter the carpet. Syringes with needles fixed and blood inside discarded like the junkies lives.

On the mattress is the female. I use the description lightly as I cannot tell from the haggard gaunt face. On her left tit an infant barely days old is trying to extract milk. The female is out of it. A needle in her arm with works attached has been recently used and her head is rolling against the wall she's propped against. I've never seen such depravity as this in all my service. I feel the need to vomit but I'm in role and Treacle has a gun. I can't take my eyes from the child. She can't support the baby as her arms are dropping by her side and the child just lays on its front desperately trying to attach its mouth to her nipple.

"Wake up you fucking bitch, the kid needs feeding."

Treacle slaps her face and she turns in his direction, her pupils wide and fixed. Her mouth tries to move in response but the muscle fails as the brain can't communicate with that area of her face.

"When did she drop the kid?"

"It ain't hers. It's a mate of hers. This one had her kid taken off her at birth two days ago and she said she'd look after this kid for her mate whilst she goes out and scores. Waste of fucking time, look at her."

I can't take my eyes off her. He slaps her again and she's gone. Unresponsive. He picks the baby up by its piss-sodden babygrow and puts it in a council recycling box.

"He'll be fine in there. Come through here and feast your eyes on this lot."

He takes me through to an adjoining room. I take a look

at the baby who's on his back just staring up at the ceiling. He's breathing but listless. There's a blanket in the box. It's blue. The same used in cells at the station. I'm on my own. I've been told there is no backup and if I get caught… I don't contemplate that. My instincts have reacted with the situation I've found myself in and it must be resolved to the satisfaction of all parties concerned.

In the room are bin liners full of cultivated plants. I don't use but it smells great. Reminds me of checking the drugs safe when I did custody. Skinny man still has the gun and he's using it as a pointing prop showing me the gear. I check my watch, 1300 hours. I have no phone. To bring it in here would have been foolish. On a mantelpiece next to a water-stained picture of another child is a syringe prepped and ready to go. He must have been getting ready for a hit before I knocked. The needle is on. His back is to me and I take my opportunity. He's an easy target now he's relaxed, even with the gun. I plunge the syringe in his right bicep and push the plunger at the same time. He turns and tries to pistol-whip me but I bring my head back and away and catch his forearm, as it swings round.

He staggers and I push his hand with the gun towards his face and he drops the pistol on the floor and goes to his knees. The drugs are kicking in, his eyes are glazing then he goes. I drop him unceremoniously to the floor. I take the pistol and stick it in the crease of my back. I check it for safety before doing it. In the next room I monitor the baby's pulse. He's still alive. The other two I leave. My exit strategy hadn't involved extracting a baby in a recycling box. I pick up the crate containing the baby and move towards the door to the flat. I put him down in the hall and turn back. In the room containing the main crop I search for any other drugs. Cannabis plants aren't going to be the only drug of choice here. On the floor is a yellow box. I open it and there are twelve full strips of Gabapentin or 'gabbies', the druggie's choice of pain meds.

I find a syringe and attach a discarded needle. Back in the

kitchen I search for any fluid other than water. There's a bottle of vinegar. I draw up some vinegar to halfway in the syringe. The tablets I empty, pouring the Gabapentin powder into the works. I calculate this will amount to 21,000 milligrams as the box is full. I top the works up with bleach. The baby is asleep. I go back through the live plant room to the room containing the harvested crop and the comatose Treacle. He got his name after his propensity to eliminate competition by waterboarding rivals with a mixture of bleach and treacle to sweeten the taste.

He's spark out on the floor. Saliva is running down a ravine made by his part open mouth. I elevate his right arm and take a deep breath. I shake the syringe; it looks gritty but dissolved well. I need this to go to his heart quickly. He moans but doesn't say anything coherent. I look at my cocktail of death. He remembered me when he shouldn't have, he knows me, he treats women and children like dirt and has no respect for the elderly. I push the syringe into his bicep vein and press the plunger. In law this is classed as murder. I prefer to see it as community policing. I leave the works in. It will look better when the old bill arrive. It will be treated as suicide or murder by a rival gang. Chances of detection nil. Want or resolve to solve the crime, none.

I don't wait to see if he's dead. I need to dispose of the kid and get back to the main job. The baby is asleep. It's a good thing as he's seen enough for one day. I look through the small eyehole cut into the cloth over the kitchen window. It's purposely cut to observe the stair side of the landing. No access from the other side. It's clear. I take the crate and sleeping baby and exit left out of the flat. I shut the door. No one about. I take the stairs. It's easier descending but I try not to shake the crate around too much. I don't need a shaken baby syndrome case to explain away.

I get to the ground floor. I look at the rubbish chute. It's still full. I hear a loud diesel engine and the sound of reversing beeps. It's the council refuse team. It's bin day. I'm in luck. I take a last look at the little man. He's in a bad way but I can't drop him at a hospital, there are cameras everywhere. I'm only left with one choice. I put the container on top of the large refuse bin. It sits steadily on top of a ripped nappy bag and a rotting Indian meal. I pull my hat down and zip up my coat so the collars meet over my chin.

The refuse lorry has finished at the other block and begins reversing towards me. I exit across the road as the lorry draws level with the containers. I turn and see two men take the handles of the main bin and pull it towards the rear of the lorry. This was not meant to happen. The men attach the rear winch to the refuse bin and one of the men moves towards the lift button at the side of the truck. I turn and walk towards them as he goes to press the button. Then it happens. The button's pressed. The box wobbles precariously on top as the bin's wheels lift off the ground. I quicken my pace then the sound of the engine is muffled by a piercing mew. The man presses the emergency stop button. He lowers the bin and grabs the black crate and lifts it off.

"Hang on I think someone's dumped a kitten." The crate is lowered to the floor.

"Here Dick, someone's only gone and dumped a baby!"

I walk past the truck and, as they concentrate on the child, throw the gun into the rear of the dustcart and carry on walking. As I leave I can hear one of the men on a phone asking for an ambulance. My job here is done. The old dear can return, Lenny gets his house back and a baby gets a chance at life. I've also removed a parasite from a residential premises. I collect my phones from a council salt bin where I'd secreted them earlier. I check my messages. The screen is blank. I phone Stoner. She'll need to update Lenny on the morning's work and I need to be left alone now to prepare for the off. The gloves I keep. I'll discard them away from here.

She answers on the third ring.

"Tell Lenny his mother can move back in a couple of days. If the police ask her she's to say she was staying with a relative, which is the case. So when do I turn the other phone on? I need to know what's happening? Where I need to be. What part of the country."

I stop and pause for breath.

"You're keen ain't ya? You don't like it when a woman's in control do ya? Bet you like to take control in the sack, eh…?"

"You'll never know sweetheart. Now, when's the off?"

"I've just spoken to him as it goes. He says he'll call me back in a couple of hours. Sit tight, lover boy, until I call you later. Go and get a massage or something. You're wound up more than my coil."

With that she hangs up. I'm at a loss, I can't leave London, not that I have any intention of doing so. My work premises is out of bounds whilst I'm actively deployed and DCI Winter would shoot me rather than return the cup of tea she owes me. I need to unwind. The near miss on the baby has shaken me up. I've already killed one child and two would be too much. For the first time in two weeks I notice pain in my left leg. Today isn't the day for me to take a dive. I feel alone and it's not a good place to be.

I see an unlicensed cab and wave at him. He looks in his rearview mirror then pulls over. I jump in the back.

"Elephant and Castle, cheers."

He nods. He looks Polish, not that his place of origin matters to me. I just need to get home and pack. I won't be returning to the calm of the centre. I don't know where I will be returning to or when. Bali was the longest I've stayed in one place. The police don't really know my true address as I don't stay long enough to warrant them knowing. After this job I hope I won't be returning to London at all.

16

You can't play hardball if you don't have a pump. Hamer doesn't know it but I'll be his shadow whilst he goes about his weary way intimidating the public and generally being a prick. I chose today, as it's a designated down day by DCI Winter on account of her team's budget being over spent after two days of nothing happening. Stoner has been on another planet and I chose to stay in the city and entertain a Lithuanian barmaid. Even criminals need some time out. The drugs and guns aren't on the move as first thought. The skip lorry is still being worked on, though I don't know why.

So rather than sit or lie around I thought I'd take this time to get to know Mr Hamer a little more. I'm good like that. It's Thursday and according to Stoner he always has his lunch in the grounds of Temple . She says he likes it there as he was meant to be a lawyer but that didn't work out so he took to crime. Not much difference in my eyes. They shit on you all the same for the greatest pot of money. Most of it, the public's. I arrive at 1130 hours and take a look outside the church where he likes to take his mid-morning snack. Bang on time he turns up shuffling his fat frame towards the reinforced concrete bench. He stuffs his lardy butt down and concentrates on his Subway. He only looks up and grins when a female walks past.

I'm oblivious to him. I'm out in the open dressed casually in a black T-shirt, jeans and Converse shoes. Yes, I wear shoes. Even prosthetics are made to shoe size. I have more hair now than he would have seen me with on both my head and face. Not too much growth but enough to distort any memory of my appearance he may have stored. He doesn't take long to consume his sandwich. It was foot long but to him a light bite. He wipes his grease-stained hands and mouth with a paper napkin and with the grace of a gorilla rises from his seat and stretches. I have one eye on my book and the other on him. He starts walking towards me and his phone goes, he stops and answers it. I look down and carry on reading. He's getting closer now, ten feet if that.

"Where are you? I'm where we always meet! Where do you think I am? Hang on… I see you, I see you." He shuts the phone off and goes back to the bench and sits down.

I wonder if he's made me but have to trust my instinct that he hasn't. I'll shoot myself if I've fucked this up. I remain where I am for now. I want eyes on who's meeting him but I'm praying it's not Stoner or Ron. A male approaches him, he's around six foot athletically built with a nonchalant swagger. He's wearing a light cotton scarf despite the warmth of the day. He has the appearance of an actor but I know he's no screen artist, he's a cop paid to act like he isn't. I don't know him personally and he won't have met me. He sits next to Hamer and they shake hands. They're then joined by a shorter guy. Cop number two and clearly the boss of cop one. Hamer is on the books with the filth. Oh happy days.

I remain as neither of them is paying any interest in me. I decide to take the heat down by removing my lower limb and placing it next to me. The cops glance over, paying the same inquisitive interest as anyone else would, but carrying on the conversation with Hamer. I just look at my limb and massage the stump of my leg. Threat level reduced, just an amputee enjoying some rays. The meeting lasts about ten minutes. I can't hear what they're saying but Hamer looks twitchy. He's sweating and it isn't from the Subway. I know fear when I see it and he's an anxious man. My suspicions are confirmed when boss cop takes out a piece of paper and passes Hamer a pen and he signs it. An envelope is then passed over and it's full. I've seen full envelopes, this one cannot close, and as I bend down to put my leg back on I can see the top is open and it contains cash. I would guess around two grand. He looks about, puts it in a briefcase and gets up to leave.

He waddles past me and carries on towards the exit and out onto the street. The other two get up and walk in the opposite direction. Their counter surveillance is poor. Same route in and out. I wait until he's rounded the corner from my sight and start my follow. He doesn't look back; he's on a regular route and doesn't feel the need to be cautious. I use the cover of shops, stopping every other one and looking in the window as he carries on walking. At bus stops, I wait until he's further ahead then join the throng of Londoners grabbing their ten-minute lunch breaks. He doesn't move quickly and those he approaches move aside and let him pass. They're given no choice, either move or be moved by his pendulous gut. The heels of his shoes are worn down to the right and that's good going for a pair of Dr Martens.

As he approaches Euston Road he starts looking around. In my mind he's looking for a cab rather than anyone in particular, I move up. I need to try and hear where he's going. His right hand shoots up as he sees the For Hire sign and the black cab moves over. I take my chance. I pull down my cap over my forehead and move alongside. As it draws up I grab the back door.

"There you go, sir."

"Out of the way you bum. Driver, take me to Rosie's." I shut the door and walk off to find another cab to his location.

Rosie's. A lap-dancing club open twenty-four hours. The dancers work shifts. Eastern European women make up a good part of the trade. The club sits in a back tenement in Green Lanes, N4. This is one place not even the old bill go for entertainment. They have The Griffin. Rosie's is controlled by the Turks and they have a strict entry policy.

There's no membership, just a minimum spend of £300 a visit. That doesn't include tips for the dancers. I'm not getting in dressed like I am. I find a cafe opposite. Sit and wait. I've no way of confirming he's gone in but I have no other option right now. To attempt to go in would be suicide. If you know the place you know the dress code and it's by invite only. I know this because Stoner works this club.

The waitress brings over a Turkish coffee pot and tops me up. This place has a good mix of locals. I feel comfortable enough to stay. If I've missed him it's no big deal. This was purely for my knowledge, nothing more. My phone rings, it's Stoner. I don't answer. She can wait, she's made me wait whilst she was off her head and I've no time for snow of any kind. I look upon drugs as a scourge. A blight on society. I'd never take any. I've seen the results of what it brings. Families destroyed, kids taken into care, parents dying. I'm also pro free will so if people want it then I feel a duty to provide the purest I can. Quality control, if you will. Sugar is the legal high. Cocaine, the city's after-dinner mint.

Life's cafeteria. Same food, same menu. Drugs, the food, I'm referring to. It all comes in small meal-for-one bags. Cook over a hot spoon and enjoy. No napkins and tablecloths at this dinner, just J-cloth wipes and a body bag at the end. No change at the club's door. The bouncer has his hand over his ear to drown out traffic noise and listen to his earpiece. Every now and then he disappears inside and returns carrying a punter who he drops onto the street. Without him all you'd see is a black steel reinforced door. There's no sign for Rosie's. My phone goes again now it's DCI Winter. I ignore it. Now isn't the right time to be talking to her either.

I glance over at the door as Hamer comes out. He's hoisting his trousers and checking his fly. His cheeks flushed. He's carrying a different briefcase. My guess is he's doing the Turks' accounts. The doorman is on his phone and chatting to him. Three minutes go by and a taxi arrives. Private hire, not black cab. Hamer gets in and the cab heads off towards Islington. I'm stuck. I have no means of following him so quickly. I leave my cash on the table and exit. He'll be good for another day. I call Stoner first and see what she wants.

"What do you want?"

"A fucking word in your ear that's what I want!"

"You have my attention."

"Can't you do a simple task without fucking people off? Charlie Brown wants you dead and Pikey Paul says you're a miserable cunt."

"Well, you can't please everyone, now, can you. Is that it?"

"You not getting any? I know a few girls I can hook you up with if that will sort you out."

"I'll book a slot at the clinic shall I?"

She's laughing now. About time, I don't want to fall out with my only link. I wait for her cackles to subside whilst looking for a taxi. Green Lanes is getting busier the closer it comes to prayer time at the mosque. Getting a cab will be a problem. I head towards the train station. A police car flies by me, sirens on and lights bouncing off buildings.

"Where are you? I can't hear a thing. I need to meet up later. I'll shout you dinner if you like?"

She's shouting down the phone. Only to be heard, not in a hostile way. I fancy a decent meal.

"Okay. Where?"

"The Italian, Chapel Market, see you at nine?"

I agree. Bang goes any chance of a decent dinner. I head for home to change and freshen up. I haven't changed in two days. I call in.

"It's Sky. What's happening? Haven't heard from you."

"We've been busy, as has Guardino. Check the drop box; there's more cash there and a set of car keys. How are you?"

"Got a meet tonight with the friendly."

"Good. It won't be long now before we can all have a holiday. Call when you need to. Leave an update at the drop."

The superintendent's gone. I'm still here on the streets bouncing from one person to the next, never knowing who's working my strings. I just want to cut them loose but can't. Not yet. Back at the centre I open the envelope from the drop. It contains a USB and the usual cash and car location. The key tells me I've been given a Volvo. A joke, as they're renowned to be indestructible. I put the USB in my laptop and listen through headphones. An Italian voice speaks first, in English. The other I recognise as Charlie Brown.

"He's picked it up. Should be with the Pikey by now. Where'd you get him? He's a right gobby cunt who needs a lesson in manners."

There's laughter, then the Italian's voice: "Zara found him. He's done well so far. I only need him for this then he will be gone, do not worry. People like him are everywhere. Show them fortunes or the promise of it and they follow. You must remember I am your shepherd and will always guide the flock in the right direction but every shepherd knows some of the flock they have to lose, at some point, you understand?"

"Yeah, yeah, course I do. I trust you Big H. He just got on my tits, that's all. I trust we're good?"

"Very good, my friend. I've had word the lorry works and will carry well. We will move in the next two days. I need to call Germany first and check on the fleet. I trust all is good your end?"

"Sweeter than a chocolate factory. You tell me when and it will be ready."

"Good. Speak soon."

The call ends. I go to the sink and run the tap. War has been declared and I must prepare for battle. This sheep is not for the slaughter. I make one last call before leaving.

It rings twice.

"Winter. Batford. Meet me tomorrow morning, tea house near Vauxhall City Farm. My phone's off from now."

"You what? You just can't…"

I've hung up. I'll deal with her shit in the morning. I'm hungry. I get dressed and take a hundred pounds. It wouldn't pay to look too flush in front of Stoner. At least if she asks I can say I won it on a bet. Thankfully most of my clothing looks like it's seen better days so no problem there. It's worked well in this role but will need an upgrade when it's over. The end would appear to be in sight and I look forward to a shopping trip. I don't often invest in myself but this will be different. I've earned the right on this one. Most cops like me would fiddle expenses or misuse the company card. But I've done all that and got away with it. I've had great holidays and eaten in the best restaurants, all courtesy of the commissioner's Amex.

I was always at work, deployed on one job or another, but I chose where to eat, drink and play. All part of the role of the undercover. But it was never to be enough. Now Stoner waits to be entertained and I don't plan on paying. What I need is this job nipped in the bud.

17

I arrive early and take a look through the restaurant window. It's busy without being overcrowded so should be perfect to sit and chat. I'm conscious of the police station being around the corner, but it's late at night and there shouldn't be any coppers using it now. This would suit them for lunch but the patronage changes at this time to locals only.

I go across the road to a pub and wait for her to call. I don't like waiting in the open especially at a place I haven't chosen to meet at. Sometimes you have to go with your gut with any situation and mine is telling me I've been pushy enough and need to relax into it. I can't afford to alienate the whole firm even though, on the surface, it would appear my role is minimal. Not that my immediate bosses have any concern over my welfare. If only they took policing the capital as seriously as this side of the job, London would be safe as houses. But there's no money in policing unless you cross the line.

What I'm doing is small fry compared to what was being done thirty years ago. Extortion, blackmail, kidnapping and murder. I'm glad I wasn't signed up back then. I'd have been serving life.

She's got ten more minutes before I leave. I don't mind waiting for a woman but this is different. There will be no fucking after this meal is done. I notice all the others in the pub, some sitting alone, others in groups laughing and relaxed. I can't remember the last time I felt relaxed anywhere. Constantly looking for trouble that's followed me or waiting for it to turn up. The best advice I'd ever been given was by an old sweat van driver back in my probation. We'd turned up to a gypsy fight in a boozer in Wood Green. Tables going over, chairs being thrown along with punches and glass. I start to get out the van and he pulls me back in. He asks where I'm going and I tell him there's a fight and we need to sort it out. He just sits back, racks open the sherpa's door and lights up a fag. "Give it ten," he says, "then we'll go in."

Ten minutes pass and by now there's one man left standing, exhausted, and then he collapses. We stroll in and pile the prisoners up in the van and leave. No punches thrown, none of us injured. 'Fools rush in where wise men never go'. I've never forgotten those words.

My thoughts are interrupted by Stoner calling my phone. I look outside and see her on the opposite footway. She waves. I check around and leave the pub and we go to eat.

She's reserved a table in a private room in the back.

"C'mon, I won't bite. It's easier to talk in here."

I follow her in and sit down at the round table that dominates the room. It's a card gaming room for when the restaurant shuts. It won't be used tonight until the early hours so we have plenty of time to eat, chat and leave. Stoner has more than the usual twenty minutes. Big H has sanctioned the meal and meet-up. He wants time to be given to bring me in to what my role will be. I look at the menu and order the most expensive dishes on it. She does the same. She orders champagne.

We dispense with the formalities of phones, each of us safe in the knowledge we have an understanding as to their use or not when we meet. She appears different this evening, agitated, not as relaxed as usual. I put this down to her bender on the coke but I'm alert to the change. Villains appear on edge the closer a job comes to the off. The adrenalin is pumping and builds up until the job's done. Booze and coke are sedatives for some. Not me. The waiters make themselves busy. A gaudy purple curtain separates the room from the kitchen. The room isn't even painted. It stores produce in crates and bottles of drink from a wholesalers. Who said romance was dead?

"See you're looking at the decor? Lovely ain't it."

"No expense spared."

She's getting her champagne out of the cooler. She offers me some and I pass a glass. I'm a sucker for free champagne and as it's on Big H, I intend to drink it.

"Cheers then, lover, you're in." She raises her glass towards me and our glasses touch.

"I guess you'll be wondering what's gonna' happen?"

"Well call me old school but I think it's about time. I've done his tests on your word. I would hope you haven't broken it."

"Have I let you down yet? Well apart from the last two days but there's a reason for that. I was with him. He was partying before the job starts. Tradition he does in case it all comes on top and he goes away."

A waiter comes in and puts the food on the table, whispers in her ear as he goes.

"We're good now, they won't be back in until I shout them. Shall I be mum?"

"So. What's with the job? I need to know so I can clear a period of time where I'm not noticed. I might go on holiday, that kind of thing."

"All right. The fella you upset the other day, Charlie Brown, he's the main man for coke and heroin. He's told H he's got a hundred kilos of white in a warehouse in Germany. In another he's got fifty MAC-10s. He wants H to get them over here where he's got a buyer lined up. The loads are split. H has a fleet of skip lorries coming over from Germany. The one you took was tested for its capacity to carry and it's good to go. He wants you to drive the one with the guns on board. He'll pay you fifty thousand pounds as he knows the risk is high."

She stops to eat and I take the opportunity to evaluate

what she's said.

"When do I get the money?"

"Once the lorry is delivered. Ron will come over and give you the cash and take the lorry away."

"Where am I taking it?"

"I don't know. From here, it's all done on the day. He rings me and I ring you. You do as I tell you and go where I tell you. You'll get a call from me the night before the job. You'll be told where to go to get the lorry. You drive it to where you're told. You tell me once you're there and Ron comes over with your cash. Job done."

"So what you're telling me is you know nothing about the job?"

"I'm telling you what I know. H doesn't do pillow talk. On the day its slick though."

"How are the drugs coming over?"

"You don't need to know that. You just need to know where you fit in and how you get paid. I've told you that now so you're in and there's no backing out."

"I can just get up and walk away now. I don't get told what I can and can't do."

"You do when you are on an owe."

"I owe no one. I've done the tests he wanted and I'm here because I passed. So let's not fuck about on detail and you can tell him where to stick any notion I owe him."

"Calm down, this is his place and the waiters are loyal. In his eyes you owed him the moment he took you on. He's Italian like that. If I tell him you ain't interested I know this much, you're dead. Simple enough for you?"

I lean back and throw the linen serviette down on the table. She carries on eating and ignores the drama. She pours another two glasses of champagne.

"Don't you forget you owe me from Bali. I bailed you out of that car crash and a kicking. I owe you or him nothing."

This gets her attention and she puts down her cutlery and dabs her sweet lips with a serviette. She picks up her knife and points it at me across the table.

"Listen up, lover boy. Bali was Bali and I got you this fucking opportunity so all bets are off with me. If you're shitting yourself the job's too big then bring a change of trousers. You're on it and there's nothing you can do about it. Yeah, you may think you can disappear abroad and he won't find you, but I'm telling you his empire is global and he will find you. He'll have your head on display for all the other mugs who thought they could piss him off."

This is going well. I now know her true colours as well as his after listening to the taped conversation. I also know she has no idea I'm a cop. I don't respond straight away. My mind's on the money.

"Good. We're clear then. What's the timescale?"

She's smiling. It's a smile of relief. She didn't want to go back to him and tell him I wasn't keen. That would have resulted in the biggest pasting she'd ever had and she didn't want that any more than I wished it on her. She pours more champagne and I'm relaxed enough to know my work is done on this meeting so I imbibe with her.

"He wants everyone available in forty-eight hours. Here's a phone. Don't turn it on until I call you and tell you to. If you try and do it before, he'll know. He'll get told and we've discussed what will happen if you're off the job. Once this is live then all other lines you have go dark. You bin the phones and numbers until this job is over. I'll call you on this phone and this phone only. If you don't answer it within thirty minutes then I'll assume you've been nicked or dead. No other reasons will be accepted. What I can tell you is your lorry is here already and being prepared for you. The rest will follow on the same day yours moves."

"So I'm not trusted on the main job? I'm being given some other job whilst the main action's happening?"

"No. He likes you and how you work. Yours is the main job. You must deliver. Why do you think he's gonna pay you so well? He never pays that amount. He must really want this one perfect and that's why he's trusting I've picked the right bloke for the work. I know I have and you know it too. You not eating?"

I check my plate and realise I've barely touched it. I make up for it as we begin to relax now the formal side is done. The next forty-eight hours will be busy for me and DCI Winter. Her team will have never worked so hard. As for me I'm prepared for little sleep and pressure. My side will want a piece of me as will DCI Winter. Big H? He already has my soul – what more could he want?

The evening comes to a conclusion as the restaurant shuts. We're the last to leave. I wonder how this will end and any illusion is shattered as the lights of a cab sweep the area. Ron leans over, nods and opens the door and she gets in. I close it and they disappear.

Chapel Market is home to the homeless now. Its streets and doorways convert to an overnight room. It won't be long before the recumbents are awakened as the market traders descend and the area takes on a different role. I head for the car. I feel okay to drive. I know I am, as Stoner's toilet breaks weren't lost on the only plant getting a good feed on quality champagne. I abhor drink-drivers. They're the real criminals, along with paedophiles, but that's a given.

18

Sun is up, wind is low and the Vauxhall City Farm is coming to life. The staff prepares the residents for their day of petting and feeding. I like the farm's serenity; its natural rhythms within its urban setting. Each animal reliant on humans for help and food. No one's going for slaughter here. It's 0800 hours. My forty-eight hours have started and I'm waiting for DCI Winter to turn up, looking forward to a cup of tea, toast and tantrums.

The cafe isn't far and I cross the grass past the football court towards it. Winter's car arrives. She's sitting, her phone near her ear, animatedly waving her hand at the windscreen then grabbing the front of her hair. Her body language indicates she's pissed off. Deep joy. Her hell is about to heat up. I don't rush but sit on the grass and observe. She really needs to relax more. I've never met a more wound-up, highly-strung woman and I've met a few women. Granted, none were as driven for their chosen success as her, but all the same they had goals and achieved them.

I'm not against women. I've laid many. I'm not proud of my behaviour and every encounter has been consensual. I have a phobia as far as commitment is concerned but who wouldn't, raised in a series of dysfunctional families? Winter, I imagine, was raised well. Parents in the force and with a need to emulate success to gain parental approval. Right now she just needs a good cup of tea and a chat with me, what could be wrong with that? I'm about to find out, as she's looked up from her phone and has seen me. Let the action begin.

I hold the door open for her and she acquiesces to my gentlemanly behaviour. She picks the table amongst the many that are vacant as we're the only customers. She's dressed in her usual grey suit, black low heel shoes, hair tied back high with a black clip. I scan the menu and kick off the conversation.

"I couldn't help notice you were in a hostile negotiation on the phone. Everything okay?"

She sits back in her chair and takes the clip out of her hair and it falls around her shoulders.

"We lost the cab from an address over in Barnsbury. We've confirmed the driver and housed him. He has the cab parked on his drive right now. Where he went from Barnsbury we don't know but we do know he picked up Guardino's accountant, Hamer. It's the first time we've had opportunity to see the cab move and I know from our last conversation time isn't on our side. I guess I over-reacted. I'm tired after being woken in the early hours by you and not getting back off to sleep."

The waitress comes over and we order. It's the first civil reply from Winter, I intend to work on it. "You're right, time is running out. In fact it's a ticking bomb and the fuse has been lit. He's going to move over the next seventy-two hours. He's rounding up the cavalry and getting the wagons ready to move out. I know this because I'm driving one of them."

I pause. She needs to take this in and decide on a response. I sit back and eat an Eccles cake. I only manage a bite.

"You're doing what? Fucking driving?"

"Keep your voice down you'll disturb the waitress." She looks around at the empty seating area.

"You don't have any authority from me to pursue that course of action on my job! Who do you think you are! I told you to call me as soon as you were making progress and you clearly fucking are!"

I take another bite and use the remaining cake as a pointing tool to reinforce my words.

"I don't answer to you re my activity, that's governed by my boss. I can't keep you up to date about activity that has national security implications. We need to stop arguing and you need to come up with what you're going to do."

A crumb trail has littered the fine cloth adorning the table. Always play the national security card when you cannot justify your actions. Winter is about to explode.

"Well you can stick your bullshit up your arse. All bets are off. You've got your job and I've got mine. I intend to nail him and that's what I'm going to do. Be very aware, Batford, I will take out whoever gets in my way. You're lower than a snake's belly. I've been asking around and there's always been talk around your methodology for getting results." She takes a breath and sips tea.

"I am to understand that when you were on the Flying Squad it was a particularly troubled period. How complaints never made anything stick is beyond me. Now look at you, wrapped up in a unit that has the national security as its main objective. What has this organisation come to? Don't darken my door again until this is done. You can tell your boss what you like. From what I can see it's just you and no one else from your unit deployed, which I find strange in itself. But hey, I'm just a DCI trying to take down a major crime lord."

She finally shuts up and checks her phone. The excision from her world is a minor setback that won't be made an issue by me unless I tell my boss. I have no intention of doing such a foolish thing. I know my role and that's all I need to know. It's already into my forty-eight hours and time costs money. I get up and leave as she answers her phone. She'll regret that move when the intelligence feed she clearly has dries up. Snouts, informants, grasses, call them what you like, in the end they're only good if the cash keeps flowing. Once this job moves she's alone with her team. The same team who can't run with a black cab for ten miles.

I carry on walking towards the Thames and head for Lambeth Bridge. I put a call in en route. Mike agrees to meet me under the bridge. I may only be a DS but in my world a boss will run when the chips are down.

I wait on the bridge and look out over the river. The flow, calming and mesmerising. Thankfully no bodies have washed up today so the river traffic is light. Gulls swoop and grab at scraps left on the bridge footway. After a few minutes, more gulls appear overhead. I move, as I've been shit on enough for one day. I take the steps down and wait. He arrives out of breath having walked, hurriedly, from New Scotland Yard. It will do him good to get out of the ivory tower and experience life at the coalface. He used to be a good UCO but once you're out of the game it affects your nerve to get back in. Times change, methods change, people change.

"You took your time." He doesn't find it amusing. He's leaning on the stone wall, head down, looking like he's going to hurl. He has the body of a retired boxer who hasn't seen a rope in years. His broken nose adds to the image.

"I came as quick as I can for fuck's sake, you said you were going to jump."

"I decided against it. Tide's out."

He looks up and a smile appears on his face and we both end up laughing. Humour is essential in this line of work.

We're alone. No one hangs around here, just runners doing their day's exercise before going back behind their desks to rot in paperwork and cash.

"Job's on. I've been told I'm driving a valuable load split from the rest. Stoner says Big H trusts me and needs this load going where it's meant to without a hitch. I don't know any more other than it's all set to move in forty-eight hours. I'll go dark as he's got phones for the job."

"Good work. His phone's gone quiet. He may have killed the line, we don't know yet. You do know we can't provide backup. Those days are over and this job's too sensitive. If it comes on top, are your next of kin details up to date on the system?"

I look at him. He's serious.

"Yes. I'll have another line. I'll let you know when it's done. Someone's talking to police. Winter is getting an intel feed from someone close. Her team are active now. They know who Ron is and are concentrating on him and his cab. I'll deal with her team. I've left the car where you left it. Here's the key, I won't be needing it from here."

He hands me a padded envelope from his messenger bag.

"This is the final payment until the job's done. Once it's over we can sort out the rest. The boss sends her regards and hopes you are well. This counts as her welfare check. I'll be telling her you're fit and good to go. The drop box is gone. You know the watches for recording are no longer in use but this is new. It won't record but it will give your location if you press the side button. It's the best we can do. We can't afford to lose this one Sam. If you press it I'll get people within the area. They won't move until they've seen you and can assess what's happening. It's a last resort and we need to be covered as an organisation. Good luck."

He hands me the watch from his wrist and I put it on. I wait as he leaves. It's like he's handed me my retirement gift and best wishes all in one. There's something he's not telling me and it doesn't sit well. That's why I lied to him about my knowledge of Hamer. I don't know who's talking to who anymore. What I do know is that the lips that whisper always have a last wish.

19

All I have fits in one large canvas holdall. I have it over my shoulder and it hugs my back with a fond familiarity. There was no one to bid me farewell. I left *Crime and Punishment* for the next inmate.

I decide to wait in the Imperial War Museum. It's free and I'll be undisturbed. My phone also has good reception here. Nothing worse than waiting for an important call than realising your phone signal's poor. I'd taken the precaution of getting two extra batteries for each phone. They're charged and good to go, which is more than can be said for me.

To kill time I take in the trench exhibit. As I walk through the mock trench the sounds from a recorder invade my brain, shouts from soldiers, gunfire and explosions. My mind numbs. I don't freeze, but part of my subconscious is telling me to. A mother and child filter past me. She ushers him gently on, using her body as a shield to her son. A bad choice of exhibit I realise but this is where I am right now, in a trench waiting for the call to go over the top. As I exit the other side my Stoner phone goes.

"Switch on the other phone. Wait until you're called and given a location to go to. It will only be me talking to you so anyone else on this line, get rid of them. Speak soon."

I'm outside now. Pigeons peck around the base of a bench where I'm sitting. I've never been in this situation before in my whole career. I can do loneliness but not like this. No backup. I shut down the Stoner phone, remove the SIM and get rid of the phone in a waste bin. I don't have any other phone now. My work one went dark after my meeting with Mike my superintendent. My only support is a blonde, coke-sniffing, fuck-buddy to an Italian drug importer. I just hope my firm have the others covered.

I've been at the museum long enough. I'm not in the habit of checking my phone every five minutes like an adulterer waiting for their lover. I have no idea where I will have to go next but hope it's commutable by public transport. I take a walk out to the main road and wait for a cab. I don't wait long the driver pulls over. I open the door and get in.

"Union Jack Club, Waterloo."

I'll wait there until my call comes in. I need the feeling of the country backing me and this is the closest I can think of. My motives may not be the purest but I still have a role to play for the greater good of the economy and public health. At least that's what I'm telling myself as my ride pulls away.

<u>Decision log entry – 15th August 2020</u>

I've heard nothing from DS Batford and I cannot rely on his timeframe as we are already forty-eight hours in and nothing has taken place as far as I can ascertain.

The cab belonging to Ron has barely moved and I have officers deployed for lengthy periods of time sat around drinking coffee and playing cards.

In light of this I feel I have two options, both of which I intend to employ:

1/ Target DS Batford as he is my only hope of finding this team and establishing what he is driving, when and from where. He is now incommunicado and it is my assumption that he may have gone rogue. I have nothing to back this up with but I will try and establish this with my next option:

2/ I have arranged a meeting with his detective superintendent, Mike Hall, from SCO35 who is responsible for DS Batford. D/Supt Hall is my only point of contact with the Metropolitan Police in relation to DS Batford's deployment.

I am open-minded at this stage but cannot comprehend how the operation was evolving until Batford and his cronies became involved.

Since their inception I have:

A) Lost my intrusive surveillance authority in relation to Guardino's phone.

B) My CHIS (Covert Human Intelligence Source) handling unit have now informed me they no longer have the friendly they were speaking to on board and had to make payment for the information they had supplied.

C) My Crimestoppers information appears to be coming from DS Batford; an officer employed on this operation whom I have no contact with or any way of contacting.

D) The black cab that was being used now seems to have run out of fuel and is having a rest.

Further lifestyle work is being attempted but to no avail.

I will await the outcome of my meeting today at New Scotland Yard.

Entry complete.

20

"Wake up! Wake up!"

My head is fuzzy, my eyes barely open and I can feel heat and pain from my right ear.

"Get up off the floor and get in the shower."

I can't register my surroundings. I'm lifted easily from the floor and dragged into a bathroom. The polyester shower curtain is flung aside and I can hear the beat of the water cascading from the showerhead. My head is shoved under the flowing storm. I shut my eyes as freezing water filters into my mouth and ears and then invades the rest of my body as I'm forced under. I have no fight left. On the bath floor I see rivulets of scarlet. My blood runs from my body, fleeing attack. From where I'm bleeding I don't know.

The room fades in and out of focus and I lean against the shower wall but then the same hand that dragged me from the floor drags me out and towards a double door. The door is opened and I'm forced, naked, to the floor. I collapse. I'm the coldest I've ever been. The snow is fierce from the balcony on what must be the top floor of a block of flats as my eyes make out a horizon of lights in the distance.

My body curls up. My knees tuck under my chin and the snow becomes one with my tears. I shut my eyes and wish for death to save me from the pain and cold. My naked body already feels as tight as rigor mortis. I try and squeeze myself warm and protect my form from what may come next. I hope I'm thrown over. A quick death would be welcome now. I have no saviour, no hero to help me. Not this time. It's me against the tyrant whose face I'm yet to witness.

The doors fly open and smash me in the back where I lie. I feel a hand grab my shoulder and as I turn I see my captor's face before more cold water is thrown over my body from a steel bucket. My father smiles and laughs as he throws the empty pail on the floor and all I remember hearing is his laughter and the sound of metal spiralling on concrete trying to find grip, a slow vibration enters my body and gradually continues…please, don't wake me…please.

My eyes open. I'm lying on a single bed in the Union Jack Club. I'm fully clothed. My childhood memory evaporated. On the bedside next to me the only phone I have vibrates and the screen flashes in unison. I sit up quickly grab the phone and press the green button.

"Yes."

"Get to Luton Airport. Go to the car hire and ask for a booking in the name of Tom Davis. Once you've got the car call me on this number."

The line goes dead. I throw the phone on the bed and lie back. It's all starting. This is either my finest hour or my final hours. A combination of the two isn't an option. I grab my bags and head for Blackfriars train station and a train to Luton Airport Parkway.

The train is on time and I've taken the liberty of travelling first class. It's a fast train so should be there in around thirty minutes unless there's a jumper on the line. The door opens and a teenage couple enter my exclusive ticket area. Both are linked by the same set of in-ear headphones and iPhone. The music is some drum 'n' bass shit that pervades my silence. I sit back and let them be. I have bigger battles ahead and would have done the same years ago except my iPhone was a Sony Walkman and I would have been alone.

As we leave Kentish Town in a blur, I feel as though I may never see London again. Whether it's wishful thinking or gut instinct I'm unsure, but the feeling is there. I glance at the teenage lovers. Not a care in the world. Their only transport this train and a skateboard at the other end. I take the opportunity to have a natural and get up and head towards the middle carriage. My luggage is stowed above and hasn't anything of value in it. I'm carrying what I value.

The train's motion has me swinging between the aisle seats as I steady myself. The toilets are in the buffet car. The only thing I take in is a male, five foot ten, short-cropped hair reading a paper. It's yesterday's, as I recognise the front page. He looks in my direction then turns away, his back towards me. At his feet is a daypack. He's not travelling by air unless he's taking a very short trip, for which he isn't dressed, wearing only jeans, a North Face Gilet, black T-shirt and brown Timberland boots.

I wait outside the toilet. It's unoccupied but I'm not happy with him. Then it happens, his phone goes. He takes it out and places it to his ear. I recognise the make and colour. National Crime Agency standard issue. I'm being followed. I enter the toilet and take a piss. When I come out he's gone and a female is in his place. Similar casual dress carrying a different paper. He knows, or thinks he knows I've made him. I now know there's more than one out on me. I need to lose them between here and the airport.

I go back to my seat. I'm more alert. The carriage near mine only has a family and children in it and the kids in my carriage are just kids. She has eyes on me through the glass in the door from the buffet car. I know she's looking at me as she starts applying lipstick in a handbag size vanity mirror that is looking my way. I resist the urge to wave.

The train is making good progress with no delays. I look out the window at the M1. My attention is on plain cars with blue lights hammering up the motorway towards Luton. Nothing evident, which tells me they're either already there or using the A1 to shadow the train. This isn't what I expected. Have to think fast as we've just passed Hendon. I make a decision. I'll outrun them closer to the venue. I have to work on the assumption I know the area better than them from previous deployments.

I relax into my seat. The surveillance officer has moved position to the side of the carriage and can see me through the glass. I make it clear I'm not moving to give the appearance I'm unaware. Luton Airport Parkway will be covered by the rest of the team. Good job, I have no intention of getting off there. My heart's beating faster as the adrenaline pumps. I love this part of the job, the thrill of evasion, even if it's my own I'm fleeing from. If Winter had agreed to work with me I could have saved her all this hassle, but hey, she will learn.

We pass St Albans; the next stop will be Luton Parkway. I get my bag from the overhead rack and place it on the floor. The surveillance officer has seen this movement. I get up and sling the large holdall over my shoulder and move to the standing area where the exit doors are. She moves her hand into her coat and her lips move. She's wired and in contact with the outside team. In her pocket is the trigger to open the mic.

The train is approaching Harpenden station. I seize the emergency handle and pull it. The train slows and the driver announces that there may be a problem and he'll stop at Harpenden to assess. He doesn't mention the emergency lever. I suspect he doesn't wish to cause any unnecessary alarm. I'm in the carriage with the driver. The surveillance officer talks into her blouse. She glances in my direction. I give no indication as to an awareness of her. I wait for my moment.

The train finally stops. The doors all remain shut. The driver is on the platform and he approaches my door. He activates the door opening from the outside and enters. He knows it's my alarm pull that's been pulled. I act quickly.

"There's a woman in the buffet car, standing to the side. Dark hair, with a bag on the floor beside her. She looks nervous and keeps talking into her lapel. There's a wire going from her pocket to a round device in her hand. I've seen the wire I think she's carrying explosives to blow up this train."

The driver looks at the surveillance officer and as he does

so I jump down from the carriage and walk towards the footway. I see her in the carriage window. She's moved and is tracking me. Her mouth is moving in speech. The driver is now shouting and passengers are panicking and moving away from her. I'm on the footway over the tracks, not looking back. I see the taxi rank and head for it. No one suspicious on the platform. Winter's team aren't here. I get to the first cab whilst behind me carnage ensues. Shouting, screaming and general disarray.

"St Albans please."

The driver nods and we move off.

As I look over, passengers are hurriedly disembarking and running in all directions. I smile, sit back and enjoy the journey. I'm aware I've caused alarm and distress but it's all in the interests of the country, they just don't know it. The cab drops me in St Albans and I find an Enterprise car hire. I use my UCO fake ID and pay cash for the car. After my near miss I decide to treat myself to one of the exotic cars on a one-way hire. Range Rover, V6, 3.0L. After all, I may be on the road for some time. I don't know yet. What I do know is that I will arrive in comfort and without my car being tracked by Big H or DCI Winter.

I need this back on my terms, not Stoner's or Big H's. I wait whilst the car is brought to the booking office. I check it with the representative and forego the vehicle introduction. I've driven a few of these on other jobs and I'm aware of the car's capabilities. I don't use the Bluetooth on the in-car phone. I call Stoner direct.

"Fuck me, that was quick. You get the car?"

"I'm in it. Now where do I go?"

"Where are you now?"

"Just tell me where you want me to go next."

"Why won't you tell me where you are? What are you doing?"

"It's called self-preservation. Now I'm in the car so where do you want me to go?"

"You know I'm gonna call my contact at the car hire and

confirm you've picked up."

I pause.

"You still there or has the cat got your tongue."

"I'm still here. After all I've done, you'd call to see if I picked up the car that I'm telling you I have? Poor, that, darling – very poor. I've a good mind to fuck this whole thing off. I've seen little money for all I've done and just taken shit from you and your mob. So you either trust me or this ends. Your choice."

I look out the car window, phone to my ear. She's silent but hasn't hung up yet. It's like a lovers' tiff but without the sex after.

"You call *me* hard work? You've got a nerve after what I've done for you. You won't be complaining after all this is done and you're rolling in money. Get your arse up north, Nottingham. Stay overnight en route but be at Carlton Races car park at five a.m."

"That wasn't too hard was it?"

'That's what she said." She's back to her old self.

The line goes dead. I check my rearview mirror and move out. There's a line of traffic behind me, an irate bus driver gesticulates, as I'd purposefully cut him off. It will be anti-surveillance from here on in. I do the first roundabout twice round and then head towards the M1 and all points north. The V6 engine guns into life and I settle back for the road trip and my next unknown destination. The leather seats are pleasantly embracing and the outside temperature gauge indicates the sunroof should be open.

I've chosen the M1, as there are no ANPR cameras heading out of London. I trust no one, which I know is rich coming from a man like me. I get on at junction 10 after taking the back roads towards the airport. Enough time has passed that Winter's team will be back at a McDonalds bitching and ordering meals on the commissioner. All she's had to fund for me is this car, my lifestyle and soon-to-be five-star accommodation at Langar Hall where I'll fit in suitably, dine well and await tomorrow morning. In the interim I'll shop in Nottingham for a suit and some other less formal clothing. Needs must when you're away from your normal place of duty.

This may appear like yet another villainous deed taking the taxpayers' money on some clothes jolly but there's a purpose. 1) I need clothes. 2) I will use the corporate covert card so this will flag up to my boss, who seemingly doesn't give a shit that I'm no longer in the Metropolitan Police District but way north of it. 3) I need to pay cash for the hotel, as I don't want her or him to know exactly where I am. There's nothing worse than uninvited guests during dinner.

More importantly, I need to show I'm still alive. I have my pension to consider and I value the widows and orphans contribution I make each month from my pay. It's not much but it's the thought that counts. I check my mirrors as I pass a traffic car parked up a roadside embankment observing the northbound drivers. I note the driver; she's eating, so I relax. It reminds me to watch my speed and I set the cruise control accordingly.

As I approach junction 21A I take the opportunity of using the services before I take the next junction. I'm in lane three and increase my speed, disengaging the cruise control. The traffic is busy and I need to start my countdown as the exit is coming up and timing across three lanes of traffic is crucial if it's to appear smooth and not cause any undue alarm to the other road users. I see the three-bar traffic countdown sign and increase speed. A gap presents itself that will permit me to weave across all lanes, if I get the speed right.

I check my nearside mirror and see a lorry closing in on the inside lane. As I dip the accelerator the V6 smoothly takes over and I'm in front of the lorry and on the slip road as it passes me, blocking any following car from entering the services. Nothing has followed. I enter the car park and park up nose out. I wait and watch. No other cars come in that surveillance would be using. Caravans and mobile camper vans aren't their style. Once I'm happy I get out and grab some provisions. I need a clean phone and a map of Nottingham.

The journey to Langar Hall was uneventful. Winter clearly has no idea where I am but I'm not convinced she doesn't know more about this job. A drive gives you time to think even when you're in escape and evade mode. It has bugged me how she knew I would be on that train travelling north and she clearly had strong intelligence to have a team behind me and not Ron or Hamer. I hold this thought as I swing the Range Rover into the tree-lined drive of this beautiful boutique hotel. If it's good enough for Sir Paul Smith and Ed Miliband then it's good enough for me. My shopping trip in Nottingham was spent in one of Sir Paul's flagship stores so it's befitting that I've also booked the main room he uses when staying here. I park up and grab my luggage. Another purchase from his range, as using the army holdall would not go down well at this establishment.

I'm greeted, checked in for dinner and shown to my room. I thank the owner of the house and we chat about the room's history as they draw the curtains over the opulent bay window. I sit on the four-poster bed. Life can be a bitch sometimes.

New Scotland Yard, conference room – 15th August 2020

Detective Superintendent Hall pours the coffee.

"Not every day we have a request for a meeting from the NCA. Please sit down."

"I haven't called this meeting to shoot the breeze about policing in the twenty-first century, I've called it because you're treading on my toes. I need to know all you know."

"And what makes you think I'm prepared to do that, DCI Winter? We're in the same job but have different agendas."

"You'll do it because one of your lot is operating like he's a one-man crusader hell-bent on fucking up my long-term operation."

"I see. Well…I still can't help you I'm afraid. It's a matter of national security. I don't need to say anymore on the subject."

"In that case I'm going from here to request an audience with the commissioner who no doubt is aware of this operation and may be of more help."

"You can request an audience with the fucking Queen, love. I don't give a shit. You will get the same message from the commissioner as I'm giving you. Back off and continue with your side of the work and leave us to ours."

"I would love to but if you think causing a bomb scare in a suburban railway station is acceptable behaviour then we are not batting for the same team. I work professionally to get the job done, not like you lot who see the world as your oyster and the job's cash as your own personal bank."

"So you admit to following DS Batford then? Why may I ask are you shadowing him when he has made it clear who is running this little syndicate about? As for cash, are you making a personal complaint of misappropriation of monies, which is a criminal offence and must be investigated?"

"Yes and no. I had to tail him. We lost the cab this morning. I found out en route to you. It hasn't been back to the address we housed it at. We also had new information that he was going to pick up a vehicle at Luton Airport. I thought he may be taken by Ron and his cab but he got on the train. The last thing I expected of him was to pull the emergency stop button and make a fake report of a suicide bomber. I don't see what's so funny, detective superintendent!"

"I apologise but, if what you say is correct and I can neither confirm or deny it was him, then you have to admire the ingenuity to evade you, don't you think?"

"Confirm or deny? It was HIM! We had a direct visual identification; he even winked at the last foot officer before he pulled the switch! I had to explain to my bosses why a whole surveillance team were stood down in under an hour's deployment. Why are you not helping me here? It was you who sent him to me not me who asked for him. What will you do about him?"

"I recognise your concerns and understand the embarrassment that may have been caused by someone under my command. The truth is, he's gone dark. Until we get new contact we don't know the situation he's in but he's good and will surface. When he does I'll let you know. I cannot do any more than that and have told you too much as it is. Fact is, we are in the same job and want the same result despite our differing remits."

"Gone dark! This is a fucking joke. Undercover officers don't go dark! You said he had a cover officer and you would provide them. Where are they? I cannot believe I'm hearing this…this is just not right…something's amiss here and I don't just mean Batford. I'm so glad I left this shower of shit when I did."

"On that note, this meeting is over, DCI Winter. Do keep in touch and let me know if anything comes over the telephones. Oh – my mistake, you can't, as you don't have that facility, so your information as to the airport must be coming from someone else? Someone close? Be careful Winter. There's more at stake here than your ego and pride. You can see yourself out."

The door slams. The perfume trace fades.

"Ma'am. It's Mike. Winter's been over. She's riled. There may be fallout coming our way from her. Thought you should know in advance."

"I expected it. She's a woman on a mission. Any news from Batford?"

"He's left a trace for us by using his credit card in a Paul Smith store in Nottingham."

"What kind of trace are we talking about?"

"One thousand and twenty pounds, ma'am."

"Jesus Christ! He's going to drive a lorry not a limousine! Let me know when he calls in. It must be imminent if he's north. It fits with the phone chatter. Guardino is excited; he's still talking with Charlie Brown, everything's in place and moving closer to the UK. Let Winter run. We need her working conventionally with just her team and no other technical support, good work."

"Thank you, ma'am."

Line goes dead. Conversations are done.

21

I hate early mornings, especially mornings stuck in a hedgerow waiting for someone to arrive. I've had no further contact from Stoner and I'm taking it on face value my contact will appear as directed. There's a low mist covering the car park but that provides me with good cover to observe whoever turns up. The binoculars I have are proving useless as the mist fogs up the glass.

Dew is my enemy, soaking my trousers and jacket even though I've laid down some old cardboard to lie on that had been dumped along with a fridge. The odd rook cackles above me and circles the tarmac before landing and hopping around observing and cocking its head, listening. For what, I don't know and don't care. A yellow glare cuts the mist and the sound of a van or lorry engine breaks the silence. I duck down into the foliage and wait. The light sweeps the car park. It heads towards me as I'm in the farthest corner from the entrance. I know they aren't here for the boot sale. I left the Range Rover at the City Airport long-term parking and cabbed it here. I've learnt to be more considerate of hired and purchased property. I also needed a decent wardrobe for my new clothes and figured the car would have to do.

As it gets closer, the Iveco van's lights cut and the driver, a white male wearing a hoodie and beanie hat, steps down and kills the engine. He's not alone. The hands of a passenger throw a used McDonald's coffee mug into the front window where it comes to rest against the screen. The driver's on the phone, the car park is deserted. No other reason for them to be here other than to meet me. He terminates his call. I'm viewing all this from my hide. He's close enough to see with binoculars but not too close to hear or see me. My phone vibrates in my pocket; it's Stoner. I answer, she sounds drowsy.

"Why aren't you at the racecourse? I've been fucking woken up by your meet saying you ain't there."

"I'm here. I can see them. Who are they and why's there two of them?"

"Big H insisted on two because you're a pain in the arse and have a habit of kicking off. They will take you to your transport, that's all I know."

"I don't like it. You could have told me where and get a cab. So what's the real reason?"

"That's it. Like I've told you just meet them, you've not got long."

She's hung up. My instinct tells me this isn't good. I've no backup and no chance of getting any. If I back out now my career is screwed and my chances of early retirement diminished. I take a deep breath, grab the holdall and drag it beside me. As the driver turns in my direction I flash a torch at him and get up. He stands still. His hands are up shielding his eyes against the torchlight. I approach him slowly as his partner is also aware and looks cagey.

"I'm here to meet you. I've just taken a call following your one."

His hands go down and I'm close enough to see his scarred left cheek, part of it hidden by stubble but I'd put money on a knife injury. He opens the large rear doors to the van.

"You'd best get in then."

I look in and can see some boxes strapped each side and in the channel in the middle a piece of foam and a blanket. Scarface sees me looking. "It's the best we could do. The front's full. There's no heating but I've put a blanket in. We've got a short trip, make yourself comfortable and make sure you have a piss before we leave."

I go to throw my bag in but an arm stops me. "Open it up and tip it out." I do as I'm told. I'm too close to the end now to enter into frivolous negotiation. Scarface rummages through my clothing and puts back the transistor radio and calculator. He does the same with the binoculars. He nods at me to carry on getting in.

I say nothing and get in the van and they shut the doors. I don't want them hearing my voice anymore, unless it's the last thing they hear. They can't identify me visually as I have my hood up and a scarf around my lower face. It gets cold out in the dirt. I settle into my bed area as the engine starts up and we begin our road trip. I have to remain calm and ironically put my trust in Stoner that she's looking after me. That part I'm struggling with, the uncertainty and loss of control. On all my previous jobs I'd called the shots, the meeting venues, how I'd fit in. All that has changed. The money isn't there to provide cover officers and backup teams. My life feels expendable under this government's plans of austerity and has for the past five years. I'd like to see the prime minister sat in this van with a pair of thugs on his way to a possible date with death or prison.

They hadn't searched me, which was strange but reassuring. I could be strapped for all they knew. I do want to know what's in the boxes. These boxes don't just contain fruit. The top of the wooden crates are adorned with pictures of oranges or bananas. If anyone were to open up the doors it would look like they've been to a market and were stocking up. Stocking up with what? I am keen to find out. It would be unusual to have every box containing contraband but most firms like to hide it across platforms, in the same way a paedophile likes to put a pleasure scene in the middle of a cinema-worthy film. You start the film thinking you're watching Disney then halfway through some child is being horrifically abused. This was one area I never investigated. None of the offenders would have made it to court.

I don't expect to find that here. Drugs yes, possibly guns, but not child porn. I open the holdall as the van goes over a bump and the crates groan. I take out the radio, calculator and some gaffer tape. I switch on the torch and turn on the radio to hear static and turn on the calculator and tape it to the radio. I begin with the bottom crates and hold the radio near the crate line and run it along and over each one. It's not long before the radio beeps. There's metal amongst the fruit in a middle crate. I didn't learn how to make a metal detector in the army or the police. I learnt this whilst bored on a long-distance flight watching a kids' cartoon called Curious George about a monkey who lives with a man with a yellow hat.

I get up and loosen a strap. Not too much as I don't want them collapsing but I do need to get inside the crate's contents. I manage to move it out enough so as not to disturb the other crates. I put my hand in the middle and feel a carrier bag then on closer grip what's clearly a gun of some sort. I've no gloves left. I remove the bag and look inside. It's a MAC-10 machine pistol. The main importation has been split into smaller parcels and appears to have arrived. I put the gun back and retighten the straps. No indication of metal from any other box. I sit back and realise this has definitely begun and isn't a dummy run. I think about calling in but my instructions were clear from both sides.

We've been on the road for twenty minutes when the van takes a left turn and slows to around ten miles per hour. The speed humps are back and I feel it in my body as the van goes over them. The van takes a shallow left then comes to a stop and the engine goes off. I can hear no other traffic outside, just the sound of gulls. The rear doors are opened and it's my turn to be blinded by torchlight. It's the passengers' turn to converse.

"Get out, we're here."

I grab my holdall and shuffle towards the light. He lowers it and as my eyes adjust I can see a river. It must be the Trent. There are boats moored and as I turn round I can see a self-storage warehouse. The doors are large enough to give access to vehicles and there are three of them. The passenger motions with his torch towards the yellow door at the far end. Near to it is a shipping container. The mist is lifting now as the sun rises and begins burning it off.

I look up at a flock of gulls as they take off from the lock platform near a weir. I wish I had the same freedom. The two heavies walk towards the shipping container and open the door. In the container is a mattress, a fridge and an old electric heater. Power has been rigged up for light and heat. "You stay here until we get the call to get you. You'll be looked after for food and water, shouldn't be more than a day." Scarface is so matter of fact about my accommodation arrangement I almost feel like I've arrived at a Premier Inn.

"Very funny. Now show me what I'm meant to be driving and let's stop taking the piss."

Scarface looks at me quizzically. "I'm not taking the piss, this is the instructions we've been given, now get the fuck in the crate and shut it."

I drop the holdall and move towards Scarface. The passenger can sense danger and starts forward towards me. I stop once I'm face to face with them both.

"How in the fuck do you expect me to survive in there? I can't even have a shit. Now I bet there's a hotel up that road where I'll stay until you come and get me."

I wake up in darkness. My head is throbbing and I feel dazed. I sit up then have to immediately lie back down. I'm in the container, they've killed the power after they whacked me on the head, with what, I haven't a clue. I'm struggling to remember the event. I feel around for my bag and find the torch. They've unloaded the crates from the van and stacked them in with me. This means one thing. Whatever else is in the crates is on me if this container gets raided.

I hear sounds outside. Voices, a shuffling of feet then the sound of metal scraping and the door opens. It's bright outside. The male at the door isn't one of the men from this morning. This guy is skinny and black. His smile is a good start as he enters the container.

"How you doing? I hear you got a good whack on the head. He don't usually take prisoners, pal, you was lucky."

He laughs and motions for me to come out.

"Who are you and how did you know I was in here?"

"There's no time for chit-chat. This aint' a blind date. Your chariot awaits and I'm on a clock. Get up, grab your shit and come with me if you want to live."

His face has turned hard. He has a look that says he means what he speaks. I do as he says. As I exit, the view is across the Trent. Boats are moored close by and on the far bank. There's a lock and the sound of the water flowing fast over the weir is soothing to my head. No people about, it feels early in the day.

Mr Motivator opens the large yellow doors to the building. The motor kicks in as the doors rattle into life. He ducks under, stops them then bends down and ushers me in. There's clearly something inside he's not keen on revealing. The skip lorry I drove is parked up. It has a new livery. It's not Guardino's company name. The name isn't important. What it contains is. In the far corner is a prefab office. The two heavies from this morning are sitting in it. They glance out the window, get up and come out. Mr Motivator ushers me towards the office, the other two are now in front of me and step aside. I feel like a boxer entering the ring with my minders flanking me. This time there's no music, just the sound of feet on the floor and whistling from behind me.

I step in and the door shuts. As I turn the lock engages. The walls are bare and soundproofed. The door is thick and double-skinned. Whatever is said in here is not for outside ears. On the right hand wall is a table with an electric iron on it and a microwave. Two chairs and nothing else. I look out the treble-glazed window and the men are in a group talking, smiling then looking back at me. My heartbeat becomes prevalent to my ears then I notice the room smells of bleach. I have the feeling I've just been moved from the holding area to the torture lab. It's like Guantanamo Bay, but it's single occupancy accommodation and no orange jump suit.

The men have now finished their catch up and move back in my direction. The passenger peels off towards the main storage door and leaves Scarface and Mr Motivator heading for my door. Scarface checks through the window and motions for me to sit down. I do as instructed. The door opens and they enter. The room is feeling more like an open-top coffin with every breath. Mr Motivator is the only speaker as Scarface has the job of head of security – namely mine.

"Don't get up my man, I've been requested by the head man to have a little chat with you. He has the feelin' someone's been talking to the wrong people about his little venture and he believes that person is you. By the wrong people, I mean the filth."

I remain still. My mouth feels dry as I haven't drunk or eaten in eight hours and I'm realising my captors and hosts didn't want to avail me of that as spew stinks and is a bitch to clean up. It reminded me of spells in custody as a young gaoler when prisoners decide to smear the wall with their own shit. I remain calm by concentrating on my breath. A skill I had started learning in Bali and in the Buddhist centre. I figured if it helped them stay calm and focused there must be something in it for me. For them it's about being there for others but you can't have everything and I'll take whatever I can get.

"You're not saying much, my man. You need to start talking or I'm gonna have to start some ironing and that won't be pretty. I hate laundry unless I'm cleaning cash. So why you been talking? Is it the money?"

I attempt to get up. Scarface slides an iron bar down from his sleeve and weighs it up in his right hand. I sit back down and re-evaluate my approach. The sweat runs down my forehead and I feel my breath on my top lip. This is a good sign. Means I'm alert. The halogen lights flicker and die. A generator fires up and they go back on. I'd missed my chance in the brief darkness.

Mr Motivator opens the microwave and takes out a sealed white paper painter's suit. The type you get from DIY stores to protect clothing. I know he has no intention on decorating but he does plan on making a mess and values his apparel.

"You've got some time to start talking whilst I get dressed. I would strongly suggest you do because by the time I'm dressed in this suit and gloves I'm ready for the party and we're the only ones coming."

He's flicked the iron on and turned up the dial on the top that adjusts temperature. "The thing with ironing, especially skin, is that you start too hot and the skin comes away easy. Makes a mess of the base and clogs the steam holes. It's a bitch to clean and the ones I use ain't cheap. See this one here? Comes with its own base and is cordless. Gives me more room to move and less chance of people flailing at the lead and getting tangled up."

He's suited now and looking at me before he undoes the box of surgical gloves that have come from the microwave. I have nowhere to move. There's only one entrance and exit and two of them. Different builds but same resolve to keep me here until their work is done. I maintain my breathing and feel remarkably calm for someone about to get branded with an Indesit iron. Mr Motivator has the gloves out of the box and is drawing them through his hands. He nods at Scarface who now walks towards me.

You'd think the most sensible thing in this scenario would be to stand up and fight. Take my chances. But that's what they're expecting as they assume my guilt. I've seen others before in this situation. They quiver, beg for mercy and still end up the same way, a beaten forlorn bloodied mass of flesh. I intend to act the opposite. I have nothing to lose.

"Take off your shirt."

"I'd rather keep it on if it's all the same. It's cold in here."

"Fucking cold? Have you any idea what he's going to do with that iron unless you do as you're told and tell him what he needs to know? It's about to go fucking thermal, pal. Now get on with it."

I take off my top and watch the black guy's eyes. It's him I need to disarm, not the bearded goon. Scarface grabs my arms and takes out plastic ties from his pocket and puts them on my wrists behind my back. My shoulders wrench back as he pulls them tight together and the backs of my wrists touch. I then feel his hand on my head as he slams it into the table. I'm dizzy but not enough to black out this time. I'm aware of hot steam near my right ear and smell the burning water. I may have made an error of judgement in my approach.

22

"Ma'am you need to see this."

"What?"

"It's a piece of Crimestoppers intelligence just come in this morning. I've been working it up and it looks good."

"Since when has an analyst been given authority to work up intelligence without the proper channels being followed? You're barely out of your teens and probably still live at home with your mother. I asked for further cover on this desk and you aren't up to speed with what I expect. Now isn't the time though, I'm in a hurry."

"I took some initiative ma'am and I think you'll be pleased. The information reads:

Guardino has a skip lorry he's loaded with a large amount of cocaine and guns. It's already in the UK. It's being moved from a lockup up north today. One of the guns is hidden in a crate containing fruit."

"So what's so special about this?"

"Well, like I said, I worked this up. I had the cab index plate that Ron uses run through the ANPR team. They picked it up travelling north yesterday and it pinged up between two cameras at a place called Gunthorpe and Lowdham. It didn't go beyond Lowdham so must have stopped in that area. I spoke with an intelligence officer in Nottingham. The only place a lorry could be hidden away is at this storage yard in Gunthorpe. That's not all: Ron tripped a speed camera and this image was sent over from Notts. It shows him and a passenger in the front. Enhancement of the image shows the passenger as an Aubrey Atwood, street name of Bunsen. He's got previous for arson and GBH. Uncorroborated source information says he's used by large OCN's as a torture tool when they suspect someone's talking to police or hasn't paid a debt. An enforcer, if you will. His favoured method is using fire or an iron. He burns them slowly until they confess."

"So what's he doing in Nottingham with our man Ron and why didn't we pick up the cab leaving yesterday?'

"You stood the team down at midnight, ma'am. He returned between midnight and oh two hundred hours. From when he first picked up a camera on the A1, I estimate he left his house at around oh two thirty hours. Maybe he's driving the lorry for them?"

"Or he's being used to flush out a grass or an undercover copper. Get me the detective super for Nottinghamshire Police who covers major crime. Put them through to my office and get the team back here and prepare a briefing. They may need overnight bags."

Fucked off doesn't even begin to express my feelings right now. DS Batford is clearly a main part in this operation and could now be in imminent danger. I have no idea where he is apart from a possible location geographically. My options are:

1) Do nothing. He is not part of my operation and in interests of national security I should not get involved. I can pass the intelligence on and let D/Supt Hall manage it.

2) I can act on this information as a possible threat to life and deploy my team to the area and work with Nottinghamshire Police in locating where the cab is and "Bunsen". I can then arrest associates that may wish to talk with police and provide further leads.

My inclination is towards option 2. I have been clearly told by SCO35 to stay out of their remit and concentrate on mine. The targets mentioned have no interest markers on PNC or other systems indicating terrorism or matters that would be of interest to my 'colleagues' in the Met.

It is clear to me now that I have been lied to regarding timescales; sources that have dried up have now possibly resurfaced.

What was a simple operation for me has now turned into a farce.

I have a duty to the officer and must take steps to ensure he is not in danger.

Entry complete

23

"Now then, my son. The iron's hot and ready to be put to work. Any last requests before I get started?"

"Let me ask you something. I've done everything I've been told to do. I have one form of communication, which you now have. I've not tried to escape or make any noise when I was in your container. If you've done your homework then you will have been told how brutal I can be and yet I've been nothing but civil. You have the wrong man. The only person I speak to is on the one number in that phone. Ring it and ask. How do you know it isn't Scarface there? I got in his van and had no idea where I was going or where I am now. He had all the details. You work it out."

Mr Motivator sits with this. His face shows doubt. He's a veteran in these situations and he'll know a wrong'un when he sees one and I'm hoping I can convince him it's not me before he sets to work.

"I've not even been paid for any of the work I've done. All my money is on a positive completion of this job. So why would I want to risk it getting screwed up?"

He's moved. I can tell as the steam from the iron near my ear has gone.

"Take his trousers off."

"What?" Scarface isn't convinced of the request

"Take his trousers off. What's the problem?"

"Nothing, but you ain't done anything to his top half

yet."

"Who's been called to do this, me or you? You're the fucking tea boy, I'm the boiling kettle and if you don't get rid of his strides in two seconds time the contents of this boiling kettle are gonna rain down on you."

My belt is undone and hands claw at the top of my trousers. I resist. What man wouldn't in this scenario? My efforts are futile as a forearm crashes into the back of my neck and in a moment my trousers are down around my ankles.

Mr Motivator is the first to react.

"What the living fuck? He's got one fucking leg and the other's out of Terminator. Who the fuck are you bruv?"

"That I can answer. I'm a drifter, ex-army, got my lower leg blown off. I wear this and get my money where I can. Not many good jobs for disabled ex-servicemen."

Mr Motivator is in my eye line now. He's put the iron down and he's looking at my back. I tense. I have no idea what he plans to do and I'm in no position to respond. I wished I believed in God but as I've said I'm not a man of any faith. Who would be, with my life's luck?

"You din't get those cigarette burns in the Army though did ya? Or those skin welts or that buckle mark. It may be fading but I ain't no fool. Where your folks now?"

"Dead."

He stands in my eye line and lowers the top of his white paper suit. He then takes off his T-shirt. His skin is a mess. Burn and scold marks line his sinewy muscular physique. He turns round and his back is a criss-cross of scar tissue. He too has his version of a guardian angel tattooed on his back but, like mine, it cannot hide the pain or mask the trauma. He turns to Scarface.

"Now you. Take your top off."

"Fuck off. Just get on with it will ya, we ain't got all day and Big H wants an answer."

Mr Motivator doesn't give. He slows his words down and speaks in a monotone voice.

"Take…your…top…off."

"Alright, alright."

Scarface lets go of me but I don't move. This is about to get interesting. Me and the Motivator have a shared history but with different parents. A shared history can go a long way in the criminal world.

"You, on the table. Turn around onto your back then sit down on this chair."

He kicks a chair along the floor. I stop it with my feet, roll over and do as he asks. I slide off the table, sit up then shuffle to the chair and sit down. I'm now sitting with my hands still strapped behind my back, my trousers down and no top on. Great fun with a hooker, but not now. Scarface is stood in front of us, his lily-white unmarked skin a stark contrast to our own. He's not wearing his history. He has none to speak of.

"Now, as you know I've been sent to do a job. When I'm sent to do a job I always deliver. It's expected and I hate to disappoint clients."

Mr Motivator is pacing now and as he does he's putting his arms back in his paper suit, zipping it up and moving towards the gloves. He puts them on. I look at Scarface. He has a twitch near his right eye. I hadn't seen it before now.

"Yo, tea boy. Go hang on to my man here whilst I reheat this baby."

The iron doesn't take as long to obtain torture temperature. He lifts it from its cradle and depresses the steam button. Mist ejects from the portholes in the base. He nods at Scarface who grips me tighter. I focus on Mr Motivator's eyes and don't shift. If he carries out his act then I'm going to make sure he sees the suffering through my eyes and that it burns through his retinas and deep into his memory. He moves closer now and straddles my legs pinning them together. I can't move them to kick him in the balls. He grabs the top of my head, as my hair isn't a decent length to get a grip on. I look him in the eye and his bloodshot eyes meet mine and we lock on.

"You should have spoken earlier but I now understand why. Your funeral bruv, I need the cash, no hard feelings, eh."

I take a deep breath in and hold it as he draws the iron back with his right hand ready to punch me then he fires his blow. At the same time he pulls my head down towards his thigh. I scream with fear. My shoulders are released as I hear another agonised wail. Mr Motivator runs up my body and kicks me to the floor. As I roll onto my back I see him pressing the iron into the face of his adversary. The screaming is gurgled as heated flesh is torn away and muscle is eroded in heat. He starts smashing the iron into Scarface's head, blow after blow after blow.

Blood and strips of flesh fly off the iron's base and hits furniture and wall. I close my eyes, I've seen enough. The smell of charred skin and decay invade my nostrils. I'm reminded of a time in my probation where I was searching a house for a dead body. There were no lights and it was pitch black. I found the body on the floor in the hallway. I say I found it, my foot did, and the crunch and stench as it connected with the fetid flesh is now prominent in my mind. At least on this occasion the soon-to-be body is fresh and won't release a swarm of bluebottles. The screaming stops and all I hear is laboured breathing. It gets closer until it's at my level. Mr Motivator is sitting by me, his torso running with rivulets of sweat visible through his ripped, bloodied, paper suit. Torn apart by Scarface's desperate hands.

I sit up and lean against the wall. He comes over and produces a knife then pulls me forward as he cuts through the plastic that ties my hands. He goes to the corner where my top had been thrown and throws it over to me.

"Put this on. I'm done. The keys for the lorry are in the microwave. There's a phone in the glove box. Turn it on and wait for the call telling you where to go. He's got one last job he needs doing before you drop the lorry off. I told him I couldn't do it but he said if you were cool after this then it's yours. He'll pay you good. His fella who does his books,

Hamer, he wants rid of him. He's been talking to the filth and messing with his money. In the fruit crate in the cab is a piece. He wants it done quick, effective and tonight. Tomorrow this all ends and then it's party time. He says you'll know what to do and where to find Hamer. I'll clean up here."

I put my top on and pull on my trousers. I shuffle over to the chair and drag myself up using it for leverage.

"What made you think it wasn't me? I need to know before I go."

He looks at me as he's throwing his bloodstained paper suit in a bag. The table looks as though an autopsy has been performed on a warm body. Scarface's head is no longer. Hair on a scalp is visible, the rest is unidentifiable.

"Any man who's been through what you have would never grass. Your parents never did time because you didn't grass on them. I won't ask how they died though. Him, well he had it coming. Big H weren't happy with him and left it up to me to make a judgement call. You passed the test, he didn't. Simple. Now you better be off as I've got some cleaning up to do."

I'm way out of my depth. I grab the lorry key and stumble out of the room and into the main storage area. The skip lorry is just parked like any other vehicle would be except if it knew its fate I doubt it would let me start her up. I'm tired and drowsy. I've just witnessed a brutal murder and been issued third-party instructions to kill. I wonder just how much more Big H wants from me on this job. I was only ever meant to drive and that was it. But I know that once you're on the firm you end up the bitch of the boss until he's done with you and I've seen how he gets rid of staff.

The one thing I'm certain of is the further I'm away from here the better and I have transport laid on. I've been told no more, other than it needs moving from here. I know it's got a gun on board as I've seen it and been told why and where I come in. I also know the job of killing Hamer must be done tonight as the bigger job is for completion tomorrow. I have to assume this lorry needs packing before delivery and that's where I'm taking it next.

I enter the lorry and drop the glove box. I find the cheap Tesco's phone and turn it on. The battery is full. I scroll through the contact list and it's empty. I put the phone in the cup holder and see the signal is good. The main door is rising and daylight enters the building. I've had no time to check outside. I wait for shouts of armed police as the doors open further. There's a quiet hubbub of dog walkers on the road and the moored boats ride the current. If there are people about, then there's no armed police waiting to go.

I put on some shades that were in the driver's door well and turn right. As I get to a public car park opposite the Anchor the phone goes. It's Stoner. For the first time I'm relieved to hear her voice. There's panic in it. Something I never thought I'd hear from her.

"You alright?"

"Yes, perfectly fine. Why wouldn't I be?"

She doesn't reply immediately.

Because I haven't gone off full salvo about how since we last spoke, I'd been taken in a van by two goons, locked in a storage container, hit unconscious, made to strip and see a man's head disappear under an Indesit iron by a psychopath who made his decision based on a best guess. I await her next instructions.

"No reason, just seemed strange not speaking to ya. I had to follow instructions. The other numbers gone, this is the final one until the job's put to bed."

"Oh great, we can just chat whilst I'm on the next part of the road trip to hell."

"Sorry lover there ain't enough credit for that. Big H says to bring the lorry to the Hendon lock up. He says you've got summit else to do for him then you'll go back and pick it up and take it to the final drop off. He ain't telling me no more.
"

"Meet me at the lock up. If it all goes wrong I need you to get something to someone for me. I need to tell you in person. Just tell me you'll be there."

"Yeah, Yeah… I can do that, just call me when you're an hour away."

"Come alone and don't tell anyone."

"Okay. He's not looking for me now, Ron ain't here until tomorrow, so I can do that."

'Good, it's important so make sure you're there. See you later."

I terminate the call and turn left over Gunthorpe Bridge and head for the A1 South. I hope she turns up. The message is vital to my survival.

24

I've always loved a road trip. This is my first in a skip lorry, granted, but the view is good from this height and I'm making great time. At least they filled up the tank so getting to London won't be a problem. The inside of the lorry's cab stinks of cigarettes and is littered with small blue pens. It feels different to the one I delivered. I monitor the rear camera. I can't afford to take chances. DCI Winter could be anywhere by now and I'm certain she'll be aware of enemy movement even if that enemy is me. I take my first anti-surveillance stop at a sex shop. I don't go in but stop in the car park. If I was being followed they'd have to commit a car to follow me in. Thankfully this doesn't happen. I decide to give it ten minutes.

Ten minutes is a long time to wait to see if you're being tailed. Even longer when you know you have a weapon in a crate of fruit on the passenger seat next to you capable of firing 1,250 9mm rounds per minute. I have a full clip of thirty-two rounds in the magazine. I have a maximum range of one hundred metres and an effective range between fifty and seventy metres. You need to know your firearms, especially when one is pointed at you. I've seen first hand the chaos a weapon can cause and I've always chosen my distances carefully when confronted by one. Treacle was different; I'd fucked up on that one and was lucky to walk away. I also know that wasting a fat American sloth using this kind of hardware will bring unwarranted attention and the likelihood of civilian casualty. Know your enemy.

My enemy at this present time is my mind. I know the temptation a weapon like this can bring in the deluded mind of the criminal. I'm no criminal; I'm an undercover police officer. I'm tempted to use the phone in the shop and call in but I have to be wary of what's being monitored. I have, after all, killed and witnessed a murder all in the space of forty-eight hours. I'm now in my final hours as far as this work goes. I need completion. Like a builder working on the same project for too long. Prolonged time leads to sloppy execution.

A car enters the car park. It parks behind me nose in. This is a good sign as the exit won't be quick. It looks like a sales rep's car. Saloon, nondescript, the type and model is irrelevant. What is relevant is that the lone male is not exiting the vehicle as quickly as I would like. No other car has come in. In a flurry he checks his rearview and side mirrors, he pauses then the driver's door opens and a bespectacled, skinny, white male with wavy mousy brown hair exits. He's in his early fifties; tie neatly done but trousers don't quite meet his shoes. Like a squirrel he darts across the car park and into the shop's door. I can only imagine he's a big spender on his excursions. Loads up with porn rather than pay to view at his hotel whilst scouring the country flogging incontinence pads to the elderly and infirm. His porn habit wouldn't look good on the company bill.

My time is up. The engine's still running and the levels on the dash are good. I move off and head towards the slip road. Having a lorry this size means getting up a decent speed before entering the dual carriageway. It also means cars move away and let you out, mainly out of a desire not to become part of the metalwork. As I make my move, I glance over at a petrol station on the northbound side. Parked up is a motorcycle. The rider moves off as I exit. To anyone else they wouldn't notice. To me I know it was deliberate. The trail has a scent and I need to lose the hounds.

"Central Six Thousand, from Alpha One do you copy,
over?"

"Alpha One, this is DCI Winter, Gold Commander, go
ahead."

"We have armed units in position await further
instructions."

"Can any activity be observed at the target premises?"

"Negative. No movement observed at
this…standby…visual on ident male Bravo front of premises
carrying a black bin liner that appears full…he's placed it on
the floor near a storage container…he's opened the
container and gone in…he's out, out, out carrying a fruit
crate. Alpha One to Central Six Thousand permission to
engage, over."

"Permission granted."

"Alpha One to Charlie Five – attack, attack, attack."

"Alpha One to Central Six Thousand… Shots fired from
police unit and suspect is down, repeat suspect down, medic
on scene and dealing, ambulance on approach."

"Alpha One to Central Six Thousand… Suspect is ident
to Bravo. Bravo is dead. I repeat Bravo is dead. No firearm
in crate but bag contains body parts, head and hands on first
account."

"Central Six Thousand to Alpha One… All received.
Forensic team are on standby awaiting area secure."

Link dies. Radio silence permeates room. Only sound
heard is the sighing of voices, the hiss of screen static and
the tapping of a pen.

"Fuck it. Get the team in and secure the crime scene.
Notts can handle the shooting enquiry just make sure we
find out who's in that bag and let's hope it's not Batford."

"Yes, ma'am. One other thing. A skip lorry has been
sighted on the A1 southbound. Surveillance team engaged."

"So it may not be Batford in the bag after all."

"Let's hope it's the right lorry, ma'am. Will keep you updated and the channel is now back with us and monitoring the surveillance team."

Winter exits, her hands embracing the front of her hair. Her fingers clenched.

Decision log entry 98 – 15th August 2020

I now have a target dead in a county 126 miles from my own force area. Target shot dead by a Notts officer and they will have lead of investigation into shooting.

I have informed our complaints department as it was a joint operation and I gave the authority to engage based on the information I was given.

Helicopter view does not look good for officer involved as no apparent weapon was seen on helicopter camera.

I am of the belief that DS Batford is NOT in the bag and that he is somewhere southbound on the A1 in possession of one hundred kilos of cocaine and a number of MAC-10 machine pistols.

I cannot afford to let him out of my team's control now they have a possible sighting of him.

I have instructed the surveillance team to remain with the vehicle until a positive ID can be made. Motorcycle is deployed and observing southbound traffic.

This is my operation and a spin off from the armed operation that may lead to the recovery of evidence. I have a duty to make sure that drugs and firearms do not hit the streets of the capital.

Well that's how I see it at this time anyway.

Entry complete.

25

I've been made. It's not my worst nightmare but this may get tricky. I see the first vehicle four cars back. The car is to the centre of the road and has good visual down the line of traffic behind me. I'm in lane one and have no intention of moving lanes as yet. I need to be close to my exit as this lorry is slower than their cars and the motorcycle, which has now gone past me. His job will be visual ID then they'll know they have the right vehicle. They'll have been shown a picture of me. That's part of the setup we have now. They won't do anything with me, as they know I'm a cop and their job is to observe and report back what they see. My concern is the team who will be shadowing them. They're likely to be armed and will take me out with anyone, when they see fit.

When we had money and manpower I would have known what was happening but those days are gone. My role was clear. Infiltrate and get the job done. Recover the guns and drugs. DCI Winter had been given the same task. Results mean an increase in budget and the saving of your team. No result means no future for your team and your remit gets handed on to the victor. That's austerity for you; even in the police the rich will gain over the poor.

The same car is four vehicles back, he's not moving up on me. I take from this that he believes I'm on the same road for the duration of my journey south. I may have to change that course of action. I have a full tank of fuel but does he? Time will tell. I put on the radio and tune into

Trent FM, the news at one breaks the cab's silence and the monotonous road noise.

Reports coming in of a police shooting in Gunthorpe. Early indications are that a man has been shot presumed dead outside a storage yard near the river Trent. Passers by reported hearing police shouting then shots were heard and an ambulance responded. We'll keep you up to date as that story develops. Meanwhile a cow has blocked the A46 northbound near Newark and drivers are advised to take an alternative route.

I flick the radio off. I have the strong compulsion to burst out laughing. If that report is accurate then there's every likelihood the only witness to my presence at the yard is now dead. His driver having left and never returned, unlikely to speak to the old bill, as he was complicit in the murder. This day is getting better and better. It confirms in my mind that it's Winter's team behind me. She suspects I was at the yard but can't prove it and has sent her team up here to evaluate. She's now left with a crime scene on foreign soil and the rest of her team out on me. I hope she got more manpower. She's going to need it.

I take this opportunity to have a banana. Potassium is good for the brain and what's the point in wasting all this fruit that's sat next to me? I doubt Big H is interested in the purity levels of this produce.

The lead car has been joined by a second backup vehicle. This vehicle is shadowing on lane two and ducks back in to let others pass rather than overtake me. I was right about the first vehicle, he's running low on fuel or I'm completely delusional and paranoia has taken over. I've never been wrong in the past and that's what's saved my life.

I know one thing for certain; I cannot let them remain with me for much longer. Time isn't on my side and I need to make the next meet point alone or everything I've been through will amount to nothing. To have DCI Winter covered in glory, cocaine and cash isn't my idea of an ultimate fantasy. I cannot see her smug face talking to camera about another major bust for her team and all the kudos that goes with such an airing. No. My intention is to be up to my ears in cash and fanny, on a beach, whilst the dust settles.

In my job planning can often go awry no matter how much effort you place on organisation. There are times where opportunity presents itself and you'd be a fool not to take it. Today is thankfully one of those days. The hand carwash scheme. Hamer loves it and it suits him well. They're everywhere and thankfully the A1 is no stranger to them.

The sign states it's coming up and I see a disused garage forecourt in the distance. The advantage of sitting high. I look back; they're still in the same formation. Time for the fun to begin. I depress the accelerator and the distance between me and the vehicle immediately behind me increases. I need to give the appearance of continuing in the same direction with no intention of altering course.

The car wash approaches and I start mentally counting down the distance I have before it would be unsafe to turn at speed. The chain in the back begins to gently sway and clash into the metal uprights as the lorry's tyres engage with the uneven road surface. My pursuers are moving into the second lane to take the advantage of closing a gap. Not for any other purpose than to get a constant watch and see if any exit is coming up where I could duck out. The last thing they will be thinking is I would need the lorry washing. I wait until the last surveillance car is alongside a nearside vehicle then abruptly turn left into the garage. The other two panic and brake. The lead car carries on and the rear one ducks in and follows behind me. One way in and one way out.

I now know the lead vehicle and also know it will be waiting further up the A1 or at the very least on a bridge where it can return on south. Good luck, my A1 route is over. I can see the driver in the camera and make a point of drawing in my side mirror towards the cab. I don't want him seeing my face in it. A tanned Eastern European approaches the lorry looking confused. I'm the first in line with another car behind me. The surveillance vehicle has waited for another car to join before getting in the queue. He's now blocked in as another car joins the rear. A bacon sandwich, if you will, except I'm about to spill out the sides. The carwash attendant is below looking up and I beckon him onto the step that leads into the driver's cab so I can hear him. He does and comes flush with my open window. I leave the engine running. The growl of the diesel beast drowns our conversation.

"You want wash boss?" He's Albanian, perfect.

I produce a hundred in twenties and his eyes light up. He leans in closer and casually looks around.

"What I want is the grey Audi estate two cars back held up for as long as possible."

He doesn't look towards the car. He nods and smiles and before I hand over the money he confirms he understands the instructions.

"No problem, boss. Have safe trip."

He takes the money and puts it in the top pocket of his waterproof coat before getting down off the steps. I hear him shout to others in his native tongue. With a deftness of productivity the remaining car windscreens and windows are smeared in soap, making visibility impossible. I move off and in my repositioned door mirror I can see the driver and passenger trying to get out of their car but the amount of carwash staff around prevents this.

Water and soap is raining down upon each vehicle in line. I grab an apple from the crate and bite into it. The force of my laughter spits it all over the inside of the lorry windscreen. I erupt inside, aching pain takes over, my whole body succumbs to the ecstasy of uncontrollable joy. I'm clear. They were the only two at that point. Another wave of joy rides over me like a tsunami as I chuck the core out of the driver's window. It ricochets off the road as I exit left towards Peterborough in search of an open garage and a road map of the UK.

DCI Winter returns to the control room.

"Ma'am, the surveillance team has reported a loss on the A1 southbound."

The DC looks down as Winter approaches his desk. Her glasses come off and she throws them across the room.

"Fucking lost him? He's in a skip lorry on the FUCKING A1! It's a straight FUCKING road!"

"Yes, ma'am. The control vehicle reports he turned off abruptly into an Albanian car wash. Charlie Six believes Batford paid them to keep them there whilst he made his exit. Charlie Six reported a loss when their vehicle was covered in soap and surrounded by Albanians. Charlie Eight couldn't continue as they were running on fumes, ma'am."

"Fucking shambles. I've got a target shot and killed in Nottingham with an unidentified body, I've got no further intelligence coming in from our friendly and the undercover officer who's meant to be assisting us has gone dark with the knowledge of his unit. I've now lost the shipment that is, to all intents and purposes, with Batford heading for who knows where and I won't be taking it out or Guardino! Get me something I can work with and get it FUCKING fast! SCO35 will not get the glory for this bust!"

DCI Winter picks up her glasses and leaves the room. As the door shuts the chatter recommences.

I'm going against my better judgement and calling in. This is deep now and I need some idea about what my lot know. I load the new SIM into the phone and activate the card. I'm not in the lorry. I have to assume its bugged by Big H's mob. I would wire it up if I had it loaded up with multiple kilos of cocaine and a MAC-10. I take a sip of my takeaway coffee and dial up. It's answered on the third ring.

"It's Sky. I'm checking in."

"About time. Where in the love of fuck are you? The commander's going spare over that clothing bill. What the fuck were you thinking of, spending that kind of money?"

"Oh, glad to see you're so fucking concerned over my welfare! I've just had to shake off Winter's cronies. Why is she looking at me and not Ron or Stone or Guardino?"

"Alright calm down, it's not as bad as you think. The cab Ron uses she keeps missing and he's lying low. Guardino is out of the country. You must be the next best option to follow."

"Not as bad as I think? It's alright for you sir, sat on your arse in the cosy confines of your home but I'm out here up to my neck in shit."

"You're on the home leg, but it's good you called in now. We don't know why she's looking at you. She's been to see me and was fucked off. I gave her a pill and she went away. We've had no communication since. I'm on standby as soon as you know where the gear is I'll come and lift it. She'll never know as long as she doesn't tail you to the drop. We have to assume your lorry is fully loaded. What do you know?"

I remain resolute in telling him fuck all. He's not instilling me with confidence he has my back and I don't believe if he did he would be giving it a careful watch.

"Nothing. I picked the lorry up and now I'm here. I was told nothing about what was on it only that I've got to get to Hendon to meet Zara."

He's silent at the other end for a few seconds, then speaks.

"You know you can't get nicked. If you do, you say nothing. We're out on a limb here and it's looking like it's falling off and requiring a prosthetic, sorry, bad analogy. Phones have gone quiet. Talk of tanning shops and investments. Big H is relaxed though, laughing and chilled. Someone on his payroll has had his fingers in the till but he's got his employment termination in hand. Nothing else said. We're monitoring that side of the threat but as he threatens people all the time it's being regarded as a low threat level."

That will be me delivering the P45 then. If only he knew – my boss, not Guardino – then the threat level would be through the roof. Problem is, the whole job would be compromised, then how would I get my money? What's one more low-life's death in the bigger picture? This is what society is crying out for. This is the Big Society the Tories wished for. Criminal cleansing. People like me will be heroes in years to come, the forefathers leading the way in the clean-up revolution. Prisons will become luxury hotels for the coked-up elite to detox. The future's bright. The future's clean. As for me, I'll be far away from here.

I've noted the panic in the superintendent's voice. He knows if I get nicked the hierarchy is coming too. I've no intention of being alone in prison if it comes to that. Far better to have someone you know on the inside with you, especially a man of rank and fallibility who can petition the screws for fairer treatment. I want to know my food hasn't been pissed in, or worse. As for the commander, she'll have to take her chances.Holloway prison no longer exists.

"Don't worry, I've no intention of getting nicked. I'll call once I'm away and meet at the agreed location. You better have a good size suitcase." I hang up and get back in the lorry.

The rest of the journey was smooth. The minor detour worked well and yet it feels good to be back in the familiar surroundings of London. I can see the service yard of the industrial unit where the drop will take place. It's deserted save for a camera on the spiked metal gatepost that now moves in my direction. The gate judders as it slowly moves on its runners. I wait until it's completely across then drive in. Stoner is at the large open warehouse doors. The area appears empty. I'm glad, last thing I need is another reception committee. The engine noise increases as I drive into the lock up then subsides to an acoustic lull as I kill the engine.

Stoner appears by my door. I'm high enough to see down her low-cut blouse but human enough to notice the bruise around her right eye. Her top lip looks swollen but we're not talking Harley Street fillers. Her plump lip was hand delivered. The fruit crate is still on the passenger seat. I don't get out immediately, just fuss in the cab. I need to be as sure as I can that she's alone. She needs to be or my plan will fail. I have no intention of failing, none at all. A bang on the door and her puzzled look tells me my stalling time's up.

"What happened to you? Been chasing parked cars?"

"Ha fuckin' ha! I'm here ain't I, isn't that what matters? Come alone you said. You don't know how fuckin' hard that is when Big H has other plans or in this case has the raving hump 'cos his other plans ain't worked out the way they should."

"What do you mean they haven't worked out? What plans?"

"How the fuck should I KNOW! I just deliver messages and this eye and face is his way of delivering messages when he's fucked off."

I've overstepped the mark. For once she shows a degree of emotion. The tears in her eyes tell a thousand stories of abuse. I know all about beatings from those who are supposed to show you love. Aside from that I know she's lying as her lover is out of the country – or maybe he isn't and my lot are taking the piss with me. I'm inclined to believe her right now. Problem is you become hardened and then your own emotions get screwed up, as she's about to find out.

I'm out of the lorry. I look around and there's nothing but a cavernous space. The unit is built to house vehicles as there are parking bay lines on the floor. No other cars around and the place feels abandoned.

"Why here? What's so special about this place?"

"He used to own it. Sold it on to a wannabe car dealer but he decided there was more money in Charlie than cars. He's doing a stretch now. Didn't have the business savvy with motors let alone drugs. I thought it was the safest place. H said he'd look after it whilst your man was away. It was no trouble getting the key."

This just gets better and better. I take a deep breath and stretch. On the back of the lorry is a toolbox. I already know what's in it and now is as good a time as any to utilise its contents. Stoner is standing, arms folded across her body in a hug. Why she never dresses appropriately for the outside is beyond me. I open up the box and take out a chain and padlock. I have no idea why it's on the lorry, as I don't deliver skips, but for my purposes it works well.

"Oi, I've not gone to all this trouble so you can walk over your truck. What is it you need to tell me? I've not got all day."

I'm facing her now. She looks so pitiful. She's back to the woman she was in Bali, one of life's tarts who get taken on by what appears to be a well-meaning owner but gives a slap every now and then to show who's boss.

"Over here."

She unfolds her arms and walks towards me. Her body moves so well, a practiced routine when she approaches any man. She smiles at me and I smile back. Resistance is futile now, we're alone and I need her trust. I lean back against the truck door as she gets closer. She blows a stray strand of blonde hair from her forehead and pushes it back into place with her shades. She's against me now, her taut muscled thighs rest against my legs. She hasn't noticed I have only one, or she's being polite. Her lips are wet and red and I feel her breath against my face as she leans in towards my ear.

"You could have booked a hotel you tight bastard," she whispers.

"It would be too quiet for what I've got planned for you."

I grab the back of her hair and spin her round so she's facing the cab. The chain wraps around her neck easily and secures to the arm of the skip loader like a coiled snake around a tree branch. She starts kicking out but feels the chain tighten and stops. She can't sit down, she can only lean. If she sits she dies from strangulation. Sadly, she can still speak. For now, anyway. I stuff a rag in her mouth and tape it with duct tape from the same toolbox. I have no time to hear ranting until I've made my speech. Her eyes are wild and forehead lines begin to show – remarkably, I think, knowing that she has work done in that area. It shows me her level of hostility. A reasonable response, in the circumstances.

Once she's stopped writhing I begin.

"Some things are never clear. Instructions that on first glance look simple cannot cover the missing piece. Unless you packed it yourself you'd never know the piece was missing until you started putting it together then realise this isn't going as planned. You see, Zara, your lover has had enough. He's told you enough and now you've become what's called a liability. This job's nearly over so it's time to mop up those on the periphery who know too much. You're one of those."

She's concentrating. A good sign.

"It wasn't a chance meeting between the two of us. It was his idea all along, your lover man, Mr Big. He knows me, you see, and he knows that I'll do a good job when a job needs that final polish. It's a shame you have to go. I've enjoyed our little chats and games but you ain't the bank love, he is. The banker's called his debt in and your life is the final payment. He told me to send his love and he says you can give me a message to send him if you like."

I open the driver's door and step up. She's looking to her left but finding the chain too constricting to move her head fully. She tries grabbing at it but realises its futility. I bring out the MAC-10. I have her full attention now.

"I'm going to undo the tape and take out the rag. If you scream I will kill you. If you remain reasonable I will listen. Do you understand?"

She nods. I step forward and put my false leg nearer to her. If she kicks out at that it won't go dead on me. I count to three in my head and rip the tape. She flinches but doesn't shout. She spits on my shoe instead. I wipe it off on the bottom of her jeans.

"You fucking arsehole. I knew…I knew you weren't right…you and him were made for each other. He's having you over, don't you see it? You're his fucking patsy, his go to for the dirty work, you're a fucking mug. Go ahead kill me why don't ya. I'll be waiting for you by the pearly gates and the first thing I'll say is I told you so. I've seen many come and go like you. One minute you're here the next you've vanished. You think he's got you on a good number don't ya? You think he's got you driving the star prize, fully loaded, you stupid, stupid cunt. I'll tell you what's on that lorry, ten kilos of white, that's it. Ten fucking kilos. Why? Because you're his fall guy, he's got the old bill onto you and whilst you're being nicked the rest is coming through on another motor. Now who's the mug? You're getting nothing for all you've done for him. You'll be banged up and the filth will laud up they've taken out ten kilos and a shooter. He'll be the one laughing when he's rolling in money from selling the other hundred and ninety. So get on with it. I'm done."

I flick off the safety and hold it to her head. She looks me in the eye. She's prepared to die. Not like the kid on the estate I blew away. He had a look of fear. He couldn't even hold the gun straight due to the weight. It's a cruel world we operate in, but you can't live in fear all your life. I flick the safety back on. Now she's confused.

"How did you get here?"

"I drove…it's round the back…black Audi TT…keys are in my bag over there."

"I've got one other job then I'm back for you. I don't believe a word so you'd better come up with a plan or you're next. Remember this, I know where you live so no noise. I'm not cruel so I'm going to loosen the chains and tie you flat on the back of the lorry. Don't struggle or resist. Do you understand?"

"Yes…yeah…I get it."

"You take this time to think. You need to convince me your life is worth more than mine."

"How long will you be?"

"As long as it takes to sort out his penultimate job. You're the last on my list."

I tape her mouth and unchain her. She walks round to the back and sits on the flat plate that the skip lowers onto. She lies back flat and I chain her hands in a crucifix to the frame of the lorry. She's shivering. There's nothing I can do about it. She needs to feel the fear and decide her fate, as do I. I go through her bag and find the keys for the unit and her car. I take her phone and remove the battery. I don't want anyone locating her here.

This unit is perfect for my next move. Hopefully, by the time I return she'll have figured things out for herself and we can put this all to bed. I also know he won't have gone to the trouble of tracking my lorry. He wants nothing to do with it. As far as he's concerned it's someone else's load he's grassing on and nothing to do with him. How the mighty operate. Pass on the crumbs whilst stuffing his face with the main dish.

I use a small side door to exit. Night is drawing in. I've convinced her Big H has told me to silence her for good. Her car and the fob works, as the lights blink in recognition. I've come too far now. This is my final act. No rehearsal and no understudy. By this time tomorrow I'll be done and back to work with a nice little nest egg. I know where my money's going and who'll take care of its cleaning. I also know who will buy the drugs. Many years of this work has put me in touch with some like-minded dealers. Nothing big just keep a low profile and split the parcel up. It won't be me selling it, I'll middle the deals and give a percentage across to the ones I trust to broker it. It makes business sense and suits me.

It's taken planning to do this. I'm no fool and no puppet of this government. You can't expect coppers to roll over and sing for their supper when the top of the food chain is creaming off the readies on champagne lunches and second homes. I don't even have a place to call a home. Not that I'd want one when burglary is up eight per cent because criminals aren't coughing anymore and there aren't enough officers to attend the scene. The damage was done for me well before I joined up. Yet another failing in the system to keep kids safe from harm.

My purpose in life is to make a silk purse out of a sow's ear. Now it's time to get stitching. I get in her car and adjust the seat. The interior smells of her and brings me comfort. I say nothing and turn my phone off. I smile into the rearview mirror. If there's a camera in here I hope it's got my good side. Although there won't be much left of the car once I'm done. I start it up and head for Elephant and Castle to begin my preparation for a trip to Barnsbury and a meeting with an accountant.

I'm not doing this for Big H. None of my work has been for him, it's all been about me. You see I never killed Hamer because he'd done Big H out of a few million. No. Big H should be more careful with who he employs. Mine was purely personal. One, I hate people who knock women about. It's not my style and I don't believe in it. Two, I hate nonces of which Hamer is one. How do I know? From the sat nav I saved from the Jeep in Bali. You see a little bird told me that some fat white bloke had been out to an orphanage I taught at, asking about the kids and offering money to take one of them out for the evening no questions asked. This little bird was so concerned they phoned me so I got in the cab to make some enquiries and see if they were still hanging around. I never got as far as the orphanage, as you know. But the sat nav is a wonderful piece of technology that showed me his route for that evening.

He thinks he's clever turning up with a load of money, a wedge of Charlie and a blonde in a nice car. He looks legit. A caring sharing wealthy Yank just wanting to show an underprivileged kid a nice time. Well it's not the nice time the kid would have been expecting so that's where I come in. When I make a promise, I keep it. I'd promised to continue funding the place and keep the kids safe. You can't have dirty nonces creeping around of an evening and ruining the harmony of the home. No, that's not Balinese etiquette and not in keeping with the house rules.

I had no intention of killing him that night but things progressed. Karma, I call it. He dies and one of my old DCs who's on night duty recognises me at the crime scene. Of course once I'm in the inner cordon my DNA is everywhere. Drifting like a magic nonce-cleansing dust. It was a game changer for me but like all things in life change is ever-present. I learnt that from the Buddhists. Education is never wasted. I'm an educator. My chosen subject is life.

Her car was easy to get shot of. I did that en route. Dropped it off at a gypsy site in Wood Green and left them with the keys. Only an insane criminal would try and recover that car from them. It hadn't taken that long and the hours were well spent. This job will end and I need it to end on a positive note for me and my bosses. After all this crime has to pay or it will have been for nothing. Nothing is not an option my bosses will have. They too have expectation of reward.

The night bus back to Hendon was empty save for a couple of drunks and a nutter. They kept to themselves and I appreciated the privacy. Time to gather my thoughts. Ponder my next move. It's like a game of chess. I anticipate the opponent's move as the rules of moving drug follows a similar path. The main rule is never reaching checkmate by getting nicked by my lot. Fat chance of that in this scenario. I remind myself to keep my head in the game and not become complacent.

First light signals a new day that I want to see the end of with a shed-load of cash and my freedom intact. As for Stoner, she better have a good idea of why I shouldn't slot her when I get back. I hate liabilities and she's fast becoming one. What's another death to my current tally? Policing is changing. No one has the resources or the time to invest in what will be considered a drug land killing.

They'll find traces of cocaine in the lorry. I'll have the ten kilos for my trouble and my lot can put it down to a killing over non-payment of debt. Sad, but that's the drugs business for you. Pay up, on time and the full amount. Don't pay up or fail to show up, then you're on an owe. It's not a payday loan. The interest calculated is based on days left to live. I've seen debtors renege. It's a messy business. Messy for the mob and messy for the clean-up team.

I get off the bus at Brent Cross and carry on by foot. No one is behind me. I put the batteries back in my phone and hers. Mine is clear. Hers displays three missed calls from an unknown number. The disher of the beating, checking in. I check her phone history. Apart from the missed calls it's clean. She knows how to keep herself safe to a point. I have to decide on the level of risk she's taken to meet me. Is it risk or is it all in the master plan to get rid of me to the old bill like a stray to the pound?

I approach the site. It's a storage place full of blue shipping crates. On the far side sits the lock-up. There's no activity and only one way in and out. The old bill could be in one of the containers or in the lock-up. I've no way of knowing. Fuck it, I'm going in. The gate is easy to get over if you've got the upper body strength. The camera is still. As I move forward, sensor lights illuminate. Wherever I step lights come on. My heartbeat begins to increase. I hate the unknown, not knowing what I'm going into.

I have no other option. If I leave her here she could talk and I can't have that. Winter has an image of her. Wouldn't take long to identify her. If she puts the pressure on she could give me up on description and cover name. I wait by the side door and listen. No sound, just the engines of passing traffic from the A406. I put the key in the lock, take a deep breath and open the door.

Stoner is still where I left her. She appears asleep, her head drooped to the right and resting on her upper arm. Nothing else has changed inside. I tug the chain and she wakes with a start. I take off the tape around her mouth. Bad move.

"You're not fucking gentle at all are ya? You could see I was asleep why didn't you just brush my face rather than yank my chain! I'm not a fucking circus animal here to entertain you." Her demeanour suggests her sleep wasn't in REM state.

"I told you to have a think whilst I was gone, not grab a quick kip. You've got five minutes tops to convince me you're telling the truth. If you don't then this is where we part company and your boss can go fuck himself."

She tries to sit up but the chains prevent her. I do nothing. Comfort isn't an option for her at this stage. For all I know she could be bluffing. She knows the end game. She's been party to the pillow talk as much as the slaps. Guardino is only human. He'll need to vent his spleen and spill his thoughts and to who better than a fuck buddy he'd happily have blown away at a phone call's notice?

"Four minutes, lady, or the click of a trigger is the last thing you're going to hear."

She looks at me. Her eyes plead a lack of understanding as to our arrangement. She looks doubtful as to what she's been told by Big H and what I've told her. Life is all about choices. Some choices bring benefit, other choices misery. She already knows about poor choices. She's been making them her entire adult life. As a kid she had no choice. What child does? The only guides we have as children are the adults who care for us. The care shown is what makes us who we are today. Both myself and Stoner weren't blessed in this area but we know about choices and self-preservation and it's this intuition I'm counting on.

"Two minutes. Start talking or praying. I'M DONE!"

I open the lorry door and go under the passenger seat and retrieve the shooter. I flick the safety off, lean on the cab and focus on my watch. I don't know what I'll do if she stays silent. I haven't got it in me to end her life, yet. I look up from my watch; she has perspiration on her brow. This isn't from heat. It's like a fridge in the lock-up.

"Alright, alright, put that fucking thing down."

I do as she asks. I don't like a weapon I haven't looked after.

"It's true. All I've told you is true; he wants you nicked or dead, he don't care. He weren't gonna trust someone I met in a hotel in Bali. He used you to get the filth off his back and the main parcel through customs. He's got a couple of ports officers on his books, turn a blind eye to any motor he wants coming through. When you went to pick up that piece from the garage there was a Range Rover. That motor has the main load hidden in a false floor and in the panels. If you pierced the metal it would be like a fucking snow machine. Big H told me if I did as he asked he'd make sure I was looked after. Me own house and car and enough cash to last me a lifetime. All I had to do was make sure you drove that lorry. He knows the old bill are listening that's why he hasn't dropped his main number but made me change yours. He couldn't make it look as though he knew he was being listened to. He can't be linked to it."

I say nothing. First rule of interviewing – if the suspect's talking, don't interrupt. Sit back, listen and wait. I nod to let her know she has my attention.

"Now it makes sense he'd want you to kill me. Once I'm dead and your nicked or dead then no one will know any different. So fuck him I say. If I'm gonna die at some point then I'll make the cunt suffer. I've got the main driver's number. I'll bell him and tell him to meet me here. Change of plan. He'll do it if I tell him but you've got to trust me to speak to him. Once he's here then you can slaughter the gear and do what you want. Take the drugs and do one. I'm as good as dead but I ain't being killed by you. You owe me a chance."

She must be telling the truth. Why offer that if you're not? Nothing like a woman scorned for the revenge to flow like a river.

"Call him in. Do as I tell you and you'll have the life you were promised. Fuck with me and you'll wish we'd never met. I take it he's being shadowed?"

"Undo me then. I ain't Princess Leia and you ain't no Jabba the Hut. I want my bounty and that's it. His shadows will do as I tell 'em. They'll wait up in their usual dive until they're needed. Big H has told them he's uncontactable until the job's done. I'm the only person in control and who he will speak to for updates. He's on a new number now. As for you, you can go fuck yourself."

I undo her. We shake hands; she gets the phone from her bag and puts the call in.

28

I've pulled all-nighters before. Tonight is no exception. I know there's a long stretch ahead and I welcome dawn and the arrival of the sun to help me stay alert. My childhood and army days were good for some things. In childhood, my being awake prepared me for flight if he was in a really drunk state. In the army, it prepared me for death. Death of the one I was sent to kill, not for being killed. My death wasn't an option.

The deaths I've caused on this job were no different. It had to be done. Kill or be killed. If I hadn't wiped out Treacle, then he would have gone on to kill through dealing. Innocent mouths end up at the wrong dinner table, drugged so mummy and daddy can get their fix. It starts with a small dose of methadone and the next thing their baby is on a slab. The druggies call their drugs 'food'. It's not the type that comes with a traffic light system to inform of the nutritional benefits.

The morning scene feels fresh and alive, in complete contrast to my scene last night of acrid smoke, petrol and forensic powder. This morning's mop up will be handled by an early team. That's the beauty of the cuts. I don't need to stay on and handover. That costs money and can be done by computer. The power of technology. The replacement of jobs.

Covert policing has been under the cosh for years. What was a legitimate, lucrative intelligence tool is no sharper than a child's first food knife. The police imposed a shift system for covert officers and that's when the intelligence dried up. No intelligence means more freedom for crooks to take advantage of un-policed streets and ports. Four years on and this is all crystal clear.

It's made my life easier now the Ts are no longer crossed. The only crossing is done by senior management and that's in religious symbolism in deference to not having death come back to bite them. The Range Rover will be here soon. Stoner has slept in the lorry and I babysit her phone. No other calls have come in. Big H has more important prizes to covet, as do I.

I won't be sad to see the back of London for a while. After any big job we get a lay-down period. I take to the mattress in a different part of the world and enjoy life whilst the players carve each other up trying to work out who's the grass amongst them. Eventually they will get to me but if I've done my job, then they'll dismiss me and carry on cleansing their immediate group.

It's a decent way of clearing out the dead and making way for new blood once the trust is broken. You never shit on your own doorstep so our lives shouldn't cross paths again. I'd brought back some food and water after last night's work. I decide to wake Stoner so she can freshen up before the Range Rover arrives. She needs to look the part.

I apply the gentle touch this time. Her head is near the passenger door. The fruit crate she discarded as it's beginning to turn. I kick it away and open the door. She stirs. She's covered in my coat and seems at peace with the world. Shame really that I have to introduce her to hell. I brush her forehead and move the hair from her face. She's lying on her side in a foetal position.

"What fucking time do you call this? I was up half the night in chains. Got any coffee?"

She sits up, pulls down the internal visor and checks herself in the small vanity mirror. A surprising addition in a lorry. She checks each side of her face, ruffles her hair then looks at me.

"You look like shit. Where'd you sleep?"

"I didn't. He should be here anytime now. Call him again and see how far away he is. Whilst you're at it, tell him to bring coffee. Mine's a straight black, double shot."

I hand her the phone and she makes the call. Once she's done she hands the phone back. "I need a piss and I don't want a minder. I'll use your spare T-shirt to wipe. You'll be able to afford a clothing chain once he's arrived so I'm sure you won't mind."

She drops down and swirls my spare top in the air as she walks off towards the corner of the lockup. I turn away. I'm a gentleman after all. She returns empty-handed. "It was piss by the way. Hate to create more of a smell than there is already."

We both hear an engine at the same time and look towards the open lock-up door. Stoner goes towards the camera and the gate button. "He'll want to see me before he comes through. We call him Barclay. He does banks when he's not driving."

Game on.

The Range Rover's three-litre engine breaks the familiarity of our voices as it comes to a stop next to the truck. A white guy, early fifties with swept-back grey hair and a tanned face looks my way. He's doing what any good criminal would in the same situation. Assess the environment and the stranger before deciding on getting out, tooled up or not.

The door opens and a brown polished brogue exits the vehicle. He's a guy who keeps fit and wears his clothes well. He kisses Stoner on each cheek and squeezes her arse. She playfully grabs his face as she sticks her tongue down his throat. There's history there that Big H wouldn't approve of. No wonder he trusted her on the phone.

"Who's this?"

He's nodding in my direction.

"Sky. He's taking the risk from here, lover. Can't have

you going away if it all comes on top. What would I do with myself?"

He relaxes. She's doing a good job. He throws me the keys to the Range Rover. I throw him the keys to the lorry. Stoner is in control here. An uncomfortable feeling for me.

"Right, strip off you two, we've not got much time"

Barclay looks at her then at me. I start first. His clothes will fit me. We throw each other's clothes at one another. He sniffs my T-shirt. "Have you heard of deodorant?"

I smile and say nothing. The less I say the less he can ask. His suit fits me well, even the brown Loake Brogues. Stoner looks over and whilst Barclay looks down to pull on the Timberland work boots she looks me up and down and winks. I feel and smell fresher. Barclay loves his cologne. I never wear it. Scent is a big factor in recognition. As much as a face. You'd know if Barclay had left a room. If I'd left a room you'd be looking for a farmer. He throws me the keys and I do the same.

"Right darlin', me and you have some catching up to do. Lover boy here can do one now. Get in the truck."

Stoner doesn't look best pleased but smiles and walks over to the lorry's cab. I open the door for her and she brushes my hand as she climbs up. She needs reassurance and I can't give her any. I know what I've got to do now and she'll tell him where he needs to go next and at what time. He doesn't ask any other questions and clearly trusts Stoner enough to take instructions from her. I get in the Range Rover, exit out of the lock-up and onto the A406 towards the A1.

My work here is almost done. I haven't had chance to check the vehicle. I have to work on the information and come to a reasoned conclusion that the plan she'd described was a good one. I pull over in the first lay-by and keep the engine running. No one following me. I check the sat nav and there's Barclay's route all laid out. The route fits with the importation. He's not that good. I also have the call log data from the hands-free. Stoner's number appears, as does the last one I knew for Big H. The last one is Stoner's. He didn't check that the route alteration was correct.

I carry on north up the A1. If all this works out from here I'm the richest fucking copper in the country, if not the world. I turn off at Letchworth and find a call box. I have change and dial up. It's answered on the fourth ring.

"Hello Crimestoppers, how can I help you?"

29

Back on the road, I'm making good time. I have to if I want this to be a success. This motor's on a meter and I'm out of change. The road is heaving with fucked off commuters dragging their sorry arses into work. I've switched routes. Anyone following me needs to be confused. I plan to fuck with their minds if they are. I check my mirrors. Nothing suspicious. No vehicles shadowing me and no one on the phone wanting to know where Barclay is. By now he's up to his nuts in Stoner and she'll keep him busy for a while giving me time to get to my next point.

My next point. That's my burning issue. I have to unload 190 kilos of white before Big H sniffs a problem and starts people in motion to rectify it. It stands to reason he won't trust Stoner with the full details of where this load is headed. I wouldn't. Not when some thug could come along and rob her of it.

Payday is normally the twentieth of the month but mine has just been cashed early. I pull into a McDonald's. The area is big. I see a coach parked, unattended. I park next to it. I pop the bonnet but only for effect. I'm going under the car and need it to look like a breakdown. As I suspected the car is, as we call it in the trade, lumped up. I remove the tracking device and stick it under the coach. The magnet welds the tracker to the underside. I see nothing else under mine that would cause me concern. The tracking device isn't an old bill one. This one is factory-fitted by Big H's garage.

I shut the bonnet and get back in. Time to head north again. The phone comes alive. It's Stoner's number. I connect, wait, then her voice fills my space.

"I've not got long, Barclay's gone for a piss. He's sweet but I've had Big H on the blower and he wants to know what's happening as he can't get hold of Barclay. I've told him all's good and that I've just spoke to him and he's stuck in traffic. He's told me to make him ring him back. What do I do now?"

I pause before responding. She sounds naturally stressed in the circumstances and not speaking with a gun to her head.

"You've done good. Tell Barclay to start running and get to Newport Pagnell services. Tell him to bell you once he's there. Tell him to park the lorry in the lorry park. Tell the shadowing mob to follow him and keep him in sight. Tell them the Range Rover was a dummy and the lorry is the loaded vehicle. Once he's gone get the fuck out of there and get a train from Mill Hill to Luton Airport Parkway. Call me once you're there, but be quick."

"I'm nervous, Sky. It's all coming on top and I'm fucking scared shitless what'll happen once Big H finds out his gear is on the trot."

She's breathing hard and not in a good way. She needs reassurance and I'm struggling to connect with my empathetic side, as she's not the one sat on over a million pounds worth of cocaine. I need her cool and alert.

"Look, I know it's tough but trust me, once we're clear of London, it'll all calm down and you and me can go our separate ways a lot wealthier than you could ever have dreamed of. No man to bash you up, just you and a bag full of cash. Do as I've told you and stay in touch."

"All right. I feel better now knowing you've got some kind of plan because I've got fuck all, other than having that cunt Big H over for all the shit he's given me. I'll see you in an hour at the station."

She hangs up and I depress the accelerator and head for

our agreed location. I check the radio; no traffic reports. I press the CD button and House Of Pain's *Jump Around* spills out of the speakers. I turn it up, relax my back into the leather, move my shoulders with the song and smile.

Control Room – Central 6000

"Ma'am, another intelligence log marked urgent by Crimestoppers' desk."

The DC waves the handwritten paper log at DCI Winter who makes her way around the computer terminal to the DC's desk.

"Okay everyone, I need your attention. Listen to this report:

A skip lorry will be heading north on the M1. It will stop at Newport Pagnell services. On board the lorry are multiple kilos of cocaine. The driver won't stop long. He's setting off from North London in an hour."

She stops. The team stop writing.

"Get me SCO19 tactical firearms advisor, on the phone, now. I want a team covertly deployed to the services and get it secured quickly. Maintain radio contact with me here. Any issues I want to hear them immediately. If the skip lorry is sighted between us and the target area then I want a loose follow and constant updates. Any questions? No? Good. Get on with it."

Camera monitors fire into life with pictures of the M1 appearing on the wall. Operators scan the motorway control room cameras for any sign of the lorry. This is the beauty of having remote access to them. Voices rise in pitch as they fight one another for recognition. A stockbroker's floor would be quieter at this time. The only money being traded here is riding on a lorry.

30

She arrives, alights from the train and scans the platform. She doesn't see me. She ascends the stairs onto the covered walkway over the tracks and walks out towards the entrance. I move from my position in a cafe area and exit the building first. She can only come out one way as can anyone else following her. I stand on the top deck of the multistorey car park and watch. She's out now and has her phone to her ear and mine begins to vibrate.

"I'm here. Where are ya'? All I can see are mullah taxi drivers and it's making me nervous. I ain't getting in one of those, so you can fuck right off with that idea."

She's looking round trying to see me then a bus cuts across my line of sight. I move but still can't make her out. My heart rate increases. Has someone grabbed her? Has she gone back inside or on the bus? People waiting for the bus are calm and collected. Rucksacks and travellers the main source of business. Then she appears, a cigarette in the same hand as her phone. I breathe out.

"Look over to your right. You'll see a main road. There's an underpass. I want you to walk the length of it until you reach a flyover bridge. Go now."

She turns right from the station and walks towards the main road. I wait and watch. She's nervous and looking around. There's nothing I can do to allay this fear. I move and watch her disappear into the underpass tunnel. So far, so good. This is a route I've used before and I know it will take seven minutes at a slow pace before you reach the residential street at the end and a secluded entrance to the Luton Hoo estate. We're the only ones on the pathway. This illusion is shattered when a marked police dog van stops and parks behind a Range Rover. That Range Rover happens to be loaded with cocaine. I catch up and put my arm around her shoulder and draw her in. I lean into her neck and whisper in her ear.

"Don't say anything unless I tell you to, okay? The cop could just be parking up for a smoke."

She nods as we get to the bridge. I can't approach the car and get in straight away. Why not? Because the dog van is a search van that contains a drugs dog. That dog is out, nose to the ground, tail whirling like a windmill. We stop and face each other. She has her back to the car and I can see the cop over her shoulder. I draw her in closer. She doesn't complain and leans in. The mutt is making its way towards the line of cars and the cop is on his phone. As the dog gets to the Range Rover his tail goes berserk and he starts darting to and fro and leaping up at the door. The handler has his back to him and is looking at the floor and concentrating on his conversation.

Our breathing is in sync. I tell Stoner not to release me but just to stay as we are until I know my next move. Judging by her grip, she has no desire to break away. The cop has no idea we're connected to the car and that's a bonus. I have no intention of him having a chance find of this amount of drugs. Not on my watch. Now the dog is circling the vehicle like a collie herding a sheep. He's so interested that he starts yipping and the handler turns around. He shuts off his phone. "What you got there, boy?" He moves towards the spaniel who is now sitting by the boot with his nose on the lock, tail swishing the dust up from the road. I'm fucked. There's nothing I can do.

You can't beat a drugs dog. I've been on operations in tube stations where the dog is walked along a line of people at the top of an escalator. The guilty who are carrying don't have time to sweat as the dog's nose attaches to the pocket where the drugs are and doesn't take it out until the handler calls them off. We're not talking about a bag of weed or a bit of sniff here. This is my retirement fund. The handler is alert now and calls his dog. The dog comes to him and sits. The handler then releases the dog and the dog indicates a strong scent from the door panels and the boot by placing his nose against the boot lock and sitting still. Then it happens. The cop's radio goes and the sound of my heart beating in my ears is interrupted by a shrill voice.

"Urgent assistance, Arndale Centre, male armed with a knife."

A police officer is calling for backup and fast. The handler calls his dog off and rushes back to the van. He's off a moment later, sirens going and lights flashing.

We release and she looks at me. "I was enjoying that," she says.

"Too much drama for me. Let's go."

"Such a charmer, ain't ya?"

I take a quick look down the street and we get in the car. Despite the situation the car feels the safest place to be right now.

"Call Big H. Tell him you've had to change your phone but using the same number. Tell him you've spoken to me and I'm broken down at Newport Pagnell services. Tell him to get Ron there in case I can't fix it and need to get spares. He'll do it if you ask him. He wants me nicked so the longer he thinks I'm out the better that chance will be."

"But you ain't with the lorry, you're with me?"

"He doesn't know that. Just put the call in and leave the rest to me. If he asks about Barclay tell him you're calling him after this call. Barclay's done this so many times before, like you said. He won't think anything's wrong once he's spoken to you."

She looks at me then at her phone. She doesn't want to make the call. I don't blame her. She has a drag of a freshly lit cigarette and puts the call in. I can hear the ringing tone.

Charlie Brown answers. She speaks first.

"All right, babes. Why you on this number? Where's my man?"

"You've a fucking nerve. What's going on? He's going mental that he can't get hold of you. He's trying Barclay but he's got no signal. What the fuck's going on girl?"

"It's all fine. My phone died so I've changed it. Tell him not to go spare; it's all in hand and going good. Sky ain't though. He's broken down at a services, Newport Pagnell. He needs Ron to get up there and help him fix it."

"Fuck! Alright, I'll tell Ron to meet him there. Tell that twat, Sky, to bell Ron and tell him where to meet him. How's Barclay doing? Why is he stopped at a McDonalds? That wasn't agreed. He should be well north by now."

I hear this part and smile. The coach hasn't moved yet and Charlie Brown clearly has the role of monitoring the main load from his laptop.

"He's fine. He says he thought he saw plain clothes old bill in a car so he pulled off the motorway and laid low for a while. He'll be off soon. He'll call me when he moves. I've got it all covered. I'll bell Big H when it's at the lock-up and he can call the bank."

"Good girl, we knew you wouldn't let us down. Bell me when Ron has sorted out the patsy. "

The line goes dead. We head north.

31

1630 hours Newport Pagnell services. Shithole. The steady flow of traffic buzzes my ears at a constant speed whilst I sit in Starbucks's garden area and wait.

I clear the two empties left on the table. I don't want to give the illusion I've been waiting for some time. The large awning provides good shade and the low sun will dazzle anyone trying to look over.

The car park's full. People busying themselves in the amusements in a bid to find reprieve from the superhighway we call the M1. From where I'm seated I have a good view of the vehicles coming in and the entrance to the services. I also know where the phone box is that my meet will call me from. There are two to the right of the entrance doors.

I've made it clear to Ron. Come in, park up and call from the telephone box. I have no intention of meeting Ron. He just needs to know where the lorry is. I need to make sure he meets it though. Why am I here then? I need to make sure the lorry doesn't leave. My end of the deal has ceased. It's part of the role but you never get caught hands on. I want to be nowhere near a court if anyone gets nicked and charged. The ops team are waiting. Winter took the Crimestoppers call seriously. Two builders vans have an armed team ready to deploy. Three tactical vehicles are positioned noses out, ready to block the road and effect the arrest. I don't have a time to shine. My work is done but I'm always up for seeing the parcel in safe hands and seeing villains on the floor with shooters at their heads. Especially ones who have tried to sell me out. I have to get my entertainment from somewhere.

Winter will have the arse. You would, if you found your hundred-kilo seizure was ten kilos. Amounts and weights can get lost in translation, especially on a dodgy line. Where's the rest? That's for me to know. Man's got to have something to trade with if the other people in my firm decide to turn Queen's evidence on me.

It's getting cold now. I check my watch – 1700 hours – and bang on time the black cab turns into the car park. Ron glances towards the lorries and nods. He parks up near the Shell petrol station and gets out. Ron puts on Ray-Bans, strolls over to the phones and enters the booth. I've moved inside Starbucks now.

"Where are ya?"

"I'm having a piss. Meet me by the lorry. It's the only skip lorry there. I've left the key in the visor. Door's open, no one will bother trying to nick it."

I grab my takeaway cup, move out and up the stairs to the southbound bridge. I look through windows across at the lorry park and the lorry. I have a great aerial view. I haven't seen Barclay but I've seen the cars shadowing him. If I were Barclay I'd be having some grub and waiting for my next call from Stoner. Ron moves towards the cab. He's naturally cautious and he's looking for me or for a rival firm looking to rob him of the load. He takes a final walkabout, approaches the lorry door and pulls it open. The visor comes down and he has the keys.

He's searching for the ignition. The lorry shudders as the engine starts first time.

All I see is the smoke of car tyres as three attack vehicles get in position, blocking the lorry. All officers are deployed. Handguns drawn. Officers pointing, lips moving, shouting instructions. From where I am, I can't hear a thing. The traffic drowns out any sound. It's like I'm in an insulated booth watching a silent movie. Ron reaches behind his belt. I stop drinking. He draws a gun and points it towards police.

It's the one I recovered from the garage. I hear one shot, then a double tap and Ron is down. I guess Ron had no intention of doing time. Suicide by cop, the media call it. I down my drink and carry on over the footway to the southbound services. Stoner is in the Range Rover protecting the nest. I have the keys to the car.

I take a walk past first and Stoner is sat in the driver's seat of the Range Rover. I get in the back and give her the keys. She moves off towards the southbound carriageway.

We say nothing. She would have heard the shots. Everyone had. Her phone goes. It's Barclay. She speaks first.

"What the fuck's happening? Where are you?"

She's on speakerphone.

"The filth have been watching us. They've shot Ron. His brain's all over the lorry. What in the fuck do we do now? The lot watching me are stuck. No one can get in or out. Big H is gonna do his nut when he hears all his gear has been taken out. Someone's grassed us up. It ain't looking good for you and me babes. We haven't been nicked. What do I do now?"

I say nothing. I can't, as she shouldn't be with me. I have to trust her instinct.

"Fuck! Fuck! Fuck! Is he dead?"

"His brain's all over the fucking lorry! Of course he's fuckin' dead you stupid bitch. You're gonna have to come and scoop me up from here. I'm not going anywhere near the other motors. They could be getting lifted any minute for all we know."

"I ain't coming to you. I ain't risking a nicking either. Once they've all fucked off, call a cab and we'll meet up in a couple of days and talk it out. I'll have spoken with big H by then and he'll know what to do. He knows it won't be us, lover."

He says nothing. The only sounds are the traffic and voices from voyeurs at the scene.

"Alright. Let me know what he says after you call him. I'll meet you if he's okay with me and you."

"Speak soon."

She ends the call.

"Right, we'll go south then cut over to the A1. I need to tie up a few loose ends. Once I've sold the gear and got the money I'll call you. Only meet Barclay if you have to. If it were me, I'd call it quits now and never see him again. Drive to Mill Hill. You can get a train back to London from there."

She says no more. She's smiling and if it weren't for her shades I would say her eyes were sparkling. We're both exhausted from little sleep. Her more than me after Barclay had paid a visit. I'm content to let her drive to the A1 then I'll take over. Both sides are tucked up now and won't be thinking about us. Big H already knows there's a problem as Stoner's phone shows ten missed calls.

32

The same security guy at Tintagel House waves me through and I make my way up the stairs to the second floor. I've stored the Range Rover in a private storage facility. I can hear voices coming from the usual meeting room. I knock and enter. The commander and the superintendent are present. A woman has her back to me, looking out over the Thames. She doesn't turn to see who's come in. When she does turn, I stop.

"Sit down, Batford."

The commander speaks curtly and I stare at the female leaning against the air heaters that travel along the length of the room but no longer work.

The commander continues. "I take it you know who this is and I can dispense with introductions?" I take time to assimilate the situation before responding.

"Yes, I do. Good afternoon, DCI Winter."

"Good afternoon, Batford."

She sits herself down. The superintendent is near the door and remains so as he locks it. The commander takes the floor. It's her show and my fears are correct. She and the superintendent have turned Queen's on me.

"This conversation isn't being recorded so feel free to speak. You know DCI Winter isn't pleased with another death by police and only ten kilos of cocaine. Neither are we. We both know how much cocaine was coming over and this falls well short. As police officers, Batford, we have a duty to the public and that duty is to serve the community and keep the streets safe. So far you have managed none of this. There are two deaths and a missing one hundred and ninety kilos of cocaine."

I look at the door, still blocked, and at the windows but the height is too great to escape alive. I'm not liking the conversation.

"Fact is, Batford, we recruited you for greater things. Covert policing has taken a beating since Kennedy and his mob went dipping their wicks and impregnating half the protestor movement in the north of Britain. Cuts have taken their toll. We are operating within the bare minimum legal requirements as far as RIPA is concerned. I'm old school, Batford, and I'm aware that covert operatives are bending the rules to get results. I can live with this, to a point, but NOT where the commodity we're looking to intercept goes off the radar completely."

This just gets better and better.

I sit back in my seat. Winter says nothing.

"I have no idea what you're talking about, ma'am. I did what I was instructed and authorised to do. You're just covering your backs."

Has to be worth a shot. I need her to play her cards quickly.

The commander doesn't take a breath before responding.

"You had basic covert human intelligence source authority as commensurate with the Regulation Investigatory Powers Act. You did not have authority to evade police, commit criminal damage to vehicles, and use a covert credit card, without authority, to purchase clothing. Need I go on?"

I'm grateful she's missed out on the deaths I was party to and committed. She clearly has no idea about those or doesn't have any evidence linking me to them. I respond appropriately.

"He instructed me to go dark. He's the authorising officer for my role!" I indicate the detective superintendent. "You're just trying to cover your own dirty tracks, the pair of you. If I'm going down I'm taking you two with me. I'm saying nothing until I've called a brief. You're accusing me of criminal acts. I haven't done anything more than follow instructions and take the lorry where I was told to. I called it in when it was safe for me. She had the lorry taken out and an associate up to his neck in shit. It's not my problem he chose to pull a gun on our lot and got wasted. I saw what happened. It was a clean shot and I'll testify in court to that if you want."

She motions towards the detective superintendent who produces a flask and some canteen biscuits from a rucksack. Typical, even in these times of austerity the job can afford to put on tea and coffee at meetings. They think they have me. They've got fuck all. If they did they wouldn't be doing it this way. Winter would have me in cuffs the moment I walked through the door. I accept the coffee and take three of the twin packs of wrapped biscuits.

I blame the cuts on my demise. I look at the three wise monkeys concentrating on me in expectation of an answer. Two hundred kilos of cocaine is nothing. Two tonnes, maybe.

I put down my coffee cup as they lean in towards me.

"This is a classic case of lost in translation. The amount was the amount Winter seized. The only other possibility is that he had her running around after a poxy ten kilos when the rest was coming over without us knowing. End of."

Winter hasn't spoken and this tells me she's been instructed to say nothing as a condition of attending this meeting. She breaks this silence.

"Where is it Batford? Rather convenient you were elsewhere when the lorry gets taken out? I wouldn't put it past you to know where the main load is and keeping it for yourself or your department to claim later."

I rise from my seat, biscuit crumbs cascade to the floor from my lap.

"You fuckin' *what*? You're accusing me of drug supply? You're one bitter bitch, you know that?"

"That's enough, *Batford!*" The commander interjects but I ignore her protestations.

"You know nothing about pro-active work, ma'am. You don't even know why I wouldn't be with the fucking lorry. Why do I want to be in the evidential chain? I get the commodity to you and you take it out without me being anywhere near it. Standard operating procedure! I gave it to you on a plate. You fucked up all the way through this investigation. Get over it and move on to something smaller, like your old man's cock."

Winter moves quickly across the room and swings at my face. I duck but she's having none of it. The superintendent weighs in and gets her off me. I'm still standing with my back to her. When I look across she's seething. Her face contorted with rage.

"You need to control that temper, ma'am. It could land you in deep shit."

She says nothing and turns away from me.

"Get out Batford! You've said and done enough. I'll call you and reconvene a debrief. "

I accept the commander's authority. I walk towards the door, biscuits stuffed into my pocket. Winter will calm down and my bosses will brush her off and she'll accept whatever they tell her. You don't attack a colleague. If you do, you hope it will all go away. This one will. I like her and I've overstepped the mark. I know where I need to be now. I feel like a painter putting the final touches to a masterpiece.

I step out, walk past Thames House and head for Vauxhall tube. I already know I won't be making this journey again. Once I've collected the Range Rover, London will be a distant memory.

<u>Final log entry – 17th August 2020</u>

Operation Storm has now concluded. The final tally is:
  Ten kilos cocaine, purity unknown.
  One MAC-10 machine pistol
  One handgun
  Two dead targets, both shot by police.
  Arrests – None. Insufficient evidence to link Guardino to the importation.

  I have spoken with SCO35 and they have stated the UCO has nothing further to add that would be of significance to the operation. The UCO was NOT in control of the lorry found at the services and hadn't seen any drugs or firearms on board. The cocaine was secured in the hollow metal arms of the skip. The firearm was in a box outside the vehicle on the skip loading plate. No fingerprints were found on the drugs or weapon. Any DNA found can be argued as transfer only. This is as far as Batford is concerned.

  I am dissatisfied with the outcome of this job.

  I believe DS Batford played a greater part in the importation than was commensurate with his role.

  I do not have enough evidence to back this up and would look foolish approaching the CPS or our own Anti-Corruption Team.

  I now have two targets I will not give up on until they are arrested and serving time.
  1/ Vincenzo Guardino.
  2/ Detective Sergeant Sam Batford
  Entry complete. Full file to be prepared for archive and future operational use. I will not stop until justice is served.
  DCI Klara Winter
  National Crime Agency
  Severely fucked off.

33

Reports coming in of a gangland execution in Islington. Two people police are naming as Zara Stone and Terry Sullivan aka Barclay were discovered late last night shot in the head in a vehicle on the Barnsbury Estate. Police are not commenting, stating they are keeping an open mind as to the motivation.

I turn off the BBC World Service and look out of my safe house window at the fields beyond. Nothing here but sheep and the smell of shit. This will be my home until I'm required again. It's only been two days and my sleep hasn't returned properly. I look at the coal scuttle by the back door, it's half-empty. I put down my fourth cup of coffee. I begin to feel emotion. A feeling that has eluded me for some time. Tears form but I fight them back. I wanted Stoner to succeed in breaking away from her life of violence and abuse. I know all I did was dig her an early grave.

This is my life now, one short trip to collect fuel and empty it onto the fire. It didn't take me long to get over my angst at having the fire active. I feared the smoke from the chimney showing I was in. When you live in the middle of nowhere surrounded by a windy Scottish climate you soon get over that fear. I know it's August but the weather hasn't been kind in the north.

I only came with what I had on. I look at the suit and shoes and burst out laughing. I did what I had to do and got the job done. My phone goes. I'd left it near the window in the kitchen to get a signal. I check the number and answer.

"We got the parcel. You were spot on. Shame it was only fifty kilos but it's better than nothing. The emergency button you activated on the watch did its job well, the location was found quickly. We'll be in touch once the dust has settled."

The caller terminates.

I step out into a brisk breeze and lock the door to my safe house. My only observer is a sheep in an adjacent field. This one is separated from the flock but has an acute awareness of my presence. I click the fob to an auction purchased Land Rover Defender. I'd paid the government's cash for in a false name. The police, in turn, have doctored the Police National Computer so all aspects of the vehicle appear to check out. Once again, I'm rehearsing a lie I know nothing about, but must be prepared to relay, with assured confidence, at a moment's notice.

Before I get in the car I walk into the wood adjacent to the cottage. A roadside salt bin has been moved. It can't be seen from the road as it's covered by undergrowth. I take off the old carpet covering it, lift up the yellow lid and dig into the top layer of salt. My fingers brush the tops of wrapped rectangular blocks and I smile. I re-cover with salt before closing the lid.

I now have a new covert credit card. I hear there's a Michelin-star restaurant at a hotel nearby. Would be a shame to waste the suit and I'm hungry.

See you on the next one and don't be late.

THE END

About The Author

Educated in Nottingham, Ian left school at sixteen. After three years in the Civil Service he moved to London for a career in the Metropolitan Police. He spent twenty-seven years as a police officer, the majority as a detective within the Specialist Operations Command. A career in policing is a career in writing. Ian has been used to carrying a book and pen and making notes. Now retired, the need to write didn't leave and evolved into fiction.

Rubicon is his debut novel. He now lives in rural Scotland where he divides his time between family, writing, reading and photography.

Author's Note

For the sake of clarity I have left the National Crime Agency ranks as traditional police ranks. Although the staff work under the auspices of the civil service, with a different grading system, many are police officers who moved over when the opportunity arose and continue to do great work in keeping the UK safe. Places change, command names change and ranks come and go. By the time you read this Detective Chief Inspector will probably no longer exist and places mentioned may have disappeared or changed use. Finally, this is a work of fiction and should be enjoyed as such.

Acknowledgements

Any writers journey is never a purely solitary pursuit. I have had some fantastic support along the way and I would like to thank the following: Jane Issac, Rebecca Bradley, Louise Voss, Liz Barnsley and Karen Coles for taking the time to read through my final draft and keep me on track. My wife for having the belief in me and being my first line of defence before anyone else reads my work. Chris McVeigh, at Fahrenheit Press, for just getting it and taking the risk on a new writer. Donna-Lisa Healy for my author photo. Finally you, the reader, for taking the chance on a new name. I greatly appreciate your support.

If you enjoyed this book we're sure you'll love these other titles from Fahrenheit Press.

Sparkle Shot by Lina Chern

Jukebox by Saira Viola

All Things Violent by Nikki Dolson

Hidden Depths by Ally Rose

In The Still by Jacqueline Chadwick

36228815R00134

Printed in Great Britain
by Amazon